W9-BGG-673

Here She Is, Ms Teeny-Wonderful!

Martyn Godfrey

Cover by David Craig

Scholastic Canada Ltd.
123 Newkirk Road, Richmond Hill, Ontario, Canada

Canadian Cataloguing in Publication Data

Godfrey, Martyn.
Here she is, Ms Teeny-Wonderful!

ISBN 0-590-71482-1

PS8563.033H47 1984 jC813'.54 C84-099392-7
Pz7.G62He 1984

Copyright © 1984 by Martyn Godfrey.
All rights reserved.

No part of this publication may be reproduced or stored in a retrieval system, or transmitted in any form or by any means, electronic, mechanical, photocopying, recording, or otherwise, without written permission of the publisher, Scholastic Canada Ltd., 123 Newkirk Road, Richmond Hill, Ontario, Canada L4C 3G5.

8 7 6 Printed in Canada 1 2 3 4/9
Manufactured by Webcom Limited

Contents

To Tom Baker
with thanks for
getting me started

1
News in St. Albert

My heart was pounding like crazy and my stomach was so tight it ached under my ribs. I felt great.

I leaned back on the seat of my BMX and tried to catch the warm July breeze. I was sweating rivers beneath the old Oilers hockey helmet.

"All set, Carol?" Wally yelled.

I looked at my friend, who stood about twenty-five metres away pushing the last garbage can onto its side and into a straight line with the other five. It was the brown plastic one from Mrs. Featherstone's. I glanced at the Featherstone house to see if anyone was watching, but the back curtains were closed. Good. I didn't want anybody disturbing me in the middle of my jump, and old lady Featherstone wasn't exactly happy when we borrowed her garbage cans to do our leaps.

I gave Wally a thumbs-up sign and tightened my grip on the handlebars, turning my head quickly to check my bicycle at the same time. Not that it needed to be checked, of course; it was almost brand new. My folks had bought it for me for passing grade six two weeks before.

The BMX had changed my life. Before, I had had an old second-hand Raleigh that jumped okay but didn't have wide enough forks to take the oversized jumping wheels. Despite the handicap, I had managed to jump four side-by-side garbage cans without wiping out.

My new bike was built for jumping: strong forks, thick frame, yellow dirt tires, the whole bit. The first day I had it I cleared five cans and now, after perfecting my technique with five, I felt ready for six. Even Wally hadn't cleared six. When he tried it, he ended up with a broken nose.

I watched Wally adjusting the plank on the pile of old bricks we had assembled in the laneway. This was going to be my take-off ramp. He pushed at the plank, making sure that the tip cleared the first can.

My stomach relaxed slightly and I took a deep breath. I think I enjoy the feeling of anxiety before jumping as much as I enjoy the jump itself. This time I had lots to be anxious about. Nobody in St. Albert had cleared six cans before, not even the junior high kids. Considering how fast the bike goes and how high, the possibilities of wiping out are frightening.

Wally waved me on and I pushed hard on the BMX's left pedal. Gravel and dirt sprayed from the laneway . I let out a holler, enjoying the acceleration, and stood up to get maximum power into each pedal thrust.

Within seconds the front wheel hit the plank dead centre and the old wood groaned under my weight. I heard the bricks grating as the bike passed directly over them.

And then the front wheel was airborne, followed instantly by the rear wheel. I pulled the handlebars backward, trying to get the bike to do an in-air wheelie, knowing that would gain me extra distance when the frame started to descend.

"Go for it," Wally shouted.

I watched the dirty cans passing below me in a wonderful blur. I was waiting for Mrs. Featherstone's clean brown one so I would know I had cleared all six. I saw it, but it wasn't beneath the bike where I wanted it to be. It was in front of the lead tire and I was coming down quickly.

"Oh boy," I sighed, knowing that I had blown it, and waited for the crash. The rear wheel hit the plastic can with a dull thud and sent it rolling off to the side. Out of control, I vainly tried to hold on to the handlebars, as if the action would save me. When the front wheel smashed down, however, it twisted my hands free and sent me sprawling forward.

Fortunately I landed on my right shoulder, then went into a pathetic roll and tumbled in a maze of arms and legs down the laneway. I came to a stop on my stomach with my face looking at some healthy twitch grass.

Wally was beside me before I even knew that I had stopped rolling. "You okay?" he asked in his slow drawl.

"Don't know," I replied as I moved each of my limbs separately to make sure nothing was broken. My left wrist felt awfully tender, but I was able to wiggle my fingers.

I raised myself to my hands and knees and gave my jumping buddy a big smile. "Almost made it," I commented.

"Sure did, Carol," he nodded. "And you almost broke your neck too. I told you, you should have built another pile of bricks and made the ramp longer."

I hate comments like that. "Help me up."

Wally grabbed my left arm and pulled. I let out a yell when he touched my wrist.

"Better let a doctor see that," he suggested.

"It's okay." I waved off his concern.

"That's what I thought when I broke my nose," he said. "I thought it was all right until I woke up with blood all over my —"

"Save me the details," I interrupted quickly.

I walked to my bike to check it out for damage. There was none. One thing about good jumping bikes, and my BMX is one of the best, they sure can take abuse.

"You're bleeding," Wally said. "There's blood on your cheek."

I touched both cheeks, trying to find what he was talking about. Again my left side had taken the punishment—I felt a tiny scrape beneath my eye.

"Carol!" The scream carried all the way down the laneway. "Carol!"

"What's that?" Wally asked.

"Sounds like my mother," I said.

"Carol!" Another scream.

"I've never heard your mom sound like that before," Wally pointed out.

"Me neither," I said with concern.

As she got a little closer I was relieved to see that she was screaming with excitement. Her smile seemed to cover her whole face as she waved a piece of paper in our direction. We stood motionless, watching her plump figure move with amazing swiftness toward our jumping ramp.

"You okay, Mrs. Weatherspoon?" Wally asked as Mom panted to a stop.

"Oh yes," she began squeaking. "Oh yes. Oh, definitely yes."

"We won the lotto?" I blurted out, wondering what else would make a thirty-eight-year-old woman get silly. I started to think of all the wonderful things I could do with a million dollars.

"No, no," Mom wheezed, deflating my thoughts

of riches. "It's better than that."

"What is it?" I said, curious to hear Mother's incredibly good news.

She waved the crumpled paper in front of my face. "Read this."

I tried to, but the paper was bouncing so much the only thing I could see was that it was a letter and that the bold purple print at the top of the page said something like "Tweety Contest." Mom must have won something.

"I can't read it," I said. "You tell me what it says. What did we win?"

"Win?" Mom scrunched her eyebrows. "Win? Oh, we didn't win anything. At least, we didn't win anything yet. Of course, I guess just getting this letter is a kind of winning. But it's not really winning. I mean, we can win a lot more than just this if you win this."

Wally was peering at me from under his long hair and I knew that he was thinking my good old mom had been soaking up too much of the hot July sun. He began backing up and I gave him the evil eye. He stopped, shrugging his shoulders.

"What are you talking about?" I asked plainly. "We're confused, Mom. Perhaps you could explain things to us?"

"Oh, I'm sorry," she giggled. I couldn't remember the last time my mother had giggled. "I'm so happy. This is probably the greatest thing that has ever happened to us."

"What is it?" I said impatiently.

"Oh Carol, we are so lucky. You've been chosen as a finalist in the Ms Teeny-Wonderful contest."

"Ms Teeny-Wonderful?" Wally said, sounding downright stupid.

"Ms Teeny-Wonderful?" I echoed, just as brightly.

Mother was grinning from ear to ear. "You know the *Canada Woman* magazine?"

Wally shook his head and I nodded.

"Well," Mother continued, "they're sponsoring a national contest for the most charming and talented girl in Canada."

"Ms Teeny-Wonderful?" I said, dumbfounded.

Mom bobbed her head. "The girl has to be between ten and thirteen years old. She can be from anywhere in the country."

Wally scratched his head.

"How can I be a finalist, Mother?" I asked. "I don't remember entering any contest, and I'm positive I wouldn't enter one with a name like Ms Teeny-Wonderful. Surely you're kidding?"

Mom was still giggling. "I entered you," she beamed. "The contest asked people to send in pictures of their favourite Teeny-Wonderful plus a sample of their talent."

"Carol doesn't have any talent," Wally said matter-of-factly.

I gave him my best dagger glare, but he didn't

notice. He just kept scratching his head.

"How does one send in a sample of talent?" I asked.

"Well, the rules explained that people should send a cassette tape of the girl singing or playing an instrument, or if she was a dancer, a list of prizes won."

It was my turn to scratch my head. I don't dance, sing or play music in any form. What did Mom tell them I did?

"What talent does Carol have?" Wally asked the question I wanted to know.

"Poetry," my mother answered, squeaking again. "Remember that poem you wrote for your language arts class last year, the one about the winter morning? I sent that to *Canada Woman*, along with the picture Uncle Clyde took of you last Christmas."

I didn't know what to say.

"The poem about winter?" Wally scratched more vigorously. "You mean that one that made the class laugh?"

"They loved it," Mom beamed proudly. "In the letter they said it was a good example of sensitive, creative writing."

Wally began to laugh and I wanted to start pounding his head. Embarrassment does that to me. Here was my mother acting like a canary in a microwave, raving about something called a Teeny-Wonderful contest, and Wally was watching the whole thing. I knew that it would be around the neighbourhood within an hour.

"What picture of me that Uncle Clyde took?" I asked, trying to sort out the facts.

"The one of you in your nightgown."

I cringed. "Save me," I whispered.

Wally was chuckling to himself. "That sure was a dumb poem," he said.

I shook my head in disbelief. "Ms Teeny-Wonderful?"

"Is Carol going to be on TV?" Wally asked.

"Of course not!" I shouted.

"Oh yes," Mother bubbled. "The Ms Teeny-Wonderful finals are going to be in Toronto. Fifty finalists from all over Canada will compete for the Ms Teeny-Wonderful crown on national TV."

"Mother!" I said, aghast.

"Carol's going to wear a bathing suit on TV like they do in all those other beauty contests?" Wally's face had a stupid grin on it.

"No," Mother explained, "she won't wear a bathing suit. But she will get to wear a fancy dress."

"Carol is going to wear a dress on TV in a beauty contest? Tough, bike-jumping Carol is actually going to be in a beauty contest and wear a dress?" Wally let out a big chuckle and began to jog away, no doubt anxious to tell the rest of the gang.

There I stood, watching my friend depart, dressed in my jeans and sweatshirt, covered in dirt and blood, holding onto the toughest jumping bike in the country and listening to my mother tell me I was going to be in a beauty contest. I could understand why Wally was so amazed at Mother's news.

2
Me . . . a beauty queen?

"Now let me get this straight," I said as I sucked violently at my can of Coke, getting a mouthful of froth. "*Canada Woman* magazine has organized a beauty and talent contest called Ms Teeny-Wonderful, for girls ten to thirteen. You sent them a picture of me plus a poem I wrote last year, and they've decided that I'm one of their finalists. And now we have to go to Toronto to be on national TV?"

My mother was taking rapid sips of her Perrier and lime. She had sunk comfortably into the sofa. "That's right. Oh Carol, you should be so proud. There were thousands of entries. To be chosen as one of the finalists is truly an honour and an opportunity."

"Truly," I mocked, flexing my sore wrist.

"They'll pay our plane fare to Toronto and put us up in the Hotel Ontario, where the contest is going to be held. Isn't it exciting?"

I belched and the Coke shot up into the back of my nose, making my eyes water. "Mom," I said, "let me ask you one question."

She smiled and saluted me with her glass.

"What in heaven's name got into you? Why on earth would you submit my name for something that sounds as stupid as a Ms Teeny-Wonderful contest?"

A cloud passed over Mom's features. For the first time since we had begun this conversation, she realized that I didn't share her silly excitement about this so-called honour.

"You're not happy?" she asked.

"A good guess," I nodded. "I am *not* happy. In fact, I am *unhappy*. I don't understand how you could have done such a terrible thing to me."

She sat up and screwed her face into a look of hurt and concern. "What's wrong, baby?" she crooned.

"Well, first, look at me. I'm dirty and I haven't even washed the blood off my face. I'm hardly what you would consider first-class Teeny-Wonderful material, am I?"

"But I think you are," she said softly.

"Mom, I only own one dress and I don't know if it still fits me. I don't care about clothes. I'm a borderline slob. I'm a tomboy. I'm not a beauty contestant."

"But I thought now that you are getting older, perhaps—"

I sighed and bit my straw. “Jeeny Carter,” I said.

“Jeeny Carter what?” Mother bit her lip.

“You should have nominated Jeeny Carter as your favourite Teeny-Wonderful. She wears skirts all the time, gets her hair done at the hairdresser’s and won’t ride my BMX because she thinks it’s too boyish.

“I’m the exact opposite. I live on my bike, I can’t do anything with my mousy brown hair and I’m skinny. I hardly have the shape to fill out fancy dresses, do I?”

“You have a nice figure,” Mother protested. “You’re slender but you’re still feminine. In fact, you’re very graceful when you walk. Your hair has a lot of potential. It’s just that you never let me do anything with it, and...”

I turned off my mind and let her rave on about the dormant characteristics that would allow me to flower into a perfect little lady.

Where did she get all this stuff from? I knew that I was a disappointment to her when I turned out to be more like a quarterback than a cheerleader. But we had had good talks about my personality and my likes and dislikes. I thought we had it all sorted out. Now I found that Mom was harbouring a secret wish to turn me into Miss Universe.

I tuned in on her words again. “...Think of how famous you’ll be in town,” she said.

“Oh great,” I gurgled through cola, picturing

Wally and the guys calling me Teeny-Wonderful.

"Think of how much fun we'll have in Toronto. You've never been to Toronto."

"But I never wanted to go to Toronto. I'm happy here in good old St. Albert, Alberta. What do I want to go to Toronto for? It's got too many people."

"You'll see the CN Tower."

"Heights scare me. So do plane rides. There's no way I can go, Mom. Not a chance."

I knew what was coming. Mother's face collapsed into a jelly-like mass. It was her how-can-you-do-this-to-me look.

I didn't let it move me. I was being very adult. "I'm sorry, Mother, but this is not what I want to do."

Tears burst from her eyes.

I was still unmoved. "Sorry."

Tears turned into blubbers. Next the coughing pleas would come.

"I just—*sob*—wanted to do—*sob, cough*—something wonderful—*cough*—for you—*cough, cough, sob*." It was a fine performance. Talk about talent.

I was still unmoved, although I had eaten half of my straw.

"There's a—*sob*—five thousand—*cough, cough*—dollar—*sob, sob*—prize."

Now I was moved. "A what?"

Mother knew she had gotten to me, because the sobbing and coughing stopped instantly. "A five thousand dollar prize, plus a trip to Disney World, plus a year's free travelling all over the country as Ms Teeny-Wonderful."

"Five thousand buckaroonies?" I said.

She nodded.

"A trip to Disney World?"

She nodded again.

"A year travelling? You mean I wouldn't have to go to school?"

Mother's head was bouncing. "No school. *Canada Woman* will pay for a tutor to help you with your lessons. But that shouldn't be more than an hour a day. Two at the most."

She was playing on my weak spots.

"I could spend the money any way I wanted? I could buy the trail bike I want?"

"You can buy the bike as long as you save some as well."

"I'll think about it," I said.

Mother jumped from the sofa, spilling her Perrier. "Oh good. I know you'll decide the right thing. And now I'm going to cook your favourite supper—lamb chops."

Boy, was I being buttered up.

* * *

I took off on my bike to find Wally. He was at the schoolyard doing bunny hops and doughnuts with his bike. I pedalled up to the wall and leaned against the school, watching him do his stuff.

Wally has a natural, easy manner on a bike, sort of like he belongs there. I always enjoy watching him jump. His slow, take-it-easy personality seems to show in his leaps. When he's climbing the ramp and sailing through midair, it seems as if he and the bike are the same thing, the same creature.

I left the wall and pedalled toward him, watching his long blond hair whip across his face as he pulled the doughnuts and laid crescents of rubber. His hair was getting so long that it covered his eyes. I wondered why it wasn't affecting his vision.

"Hey, Wal," I shouted. "Chicken Left!"

He gave me a big grin, stood up on his bike and pedalled to the far fence, where he whipped to a perfect 180° stop. I rode back to the school wall and made a less than perfect spin stop.

I looked at him in the distance, waved, saw him do the same, and pedalled toward him, building up speed quickly. Wally mimicked my action.

I always think playing Chicken is something like the old knights jousting with one another. I know a lot of people, especially parents, think that playing Chicken is stupid. My father says it's "indicative of insanity," which means it's crazy. But to Wally and me, Chicken is another test of skill, the same as jumping.

That doesn't mean there's not an element of

stupidity in it, or that it's for everybody. I wouldn't advise most of the kids I know to try it, but for us five-canners, the risks are minimal. Just enough to make it interesting.

We were both standing, pedalling at full force. I started to steer to the right and adjusted so that Wally and I were hurtling toward one another in a straight line. We closed distance rapidly, our front wheels lined up to meet dead on.

Twenty metres away I could see the grin on Wally's face. I gave the bike a couple more hard thrusts before sitting down and letting it coast toward Wally's. Again Wally mimicked my action.

Ten metres. I tightened my grip on the handlebars, feeling the pain in my left wrist.

Five metres. The bikes were on a perfect crash course.

Four metres. Get ready.

Three. Here goes.

Two. I pulled violently at the handlegrips, jerking the bike to the left. Wally, once more, did the same. We passed each other less than an arm's length away. I felt the breeze from his passing and let out a little whoop at the completion of such a fine Chicken Left.

We slowed, turned and pedalled slowly back toward each other, stopping side by side in the middle of the schoolyard.

"When are you going to get a haircut?" I panted, trying to see his blue eyes under his blond bangs.

"Long hair was in style twenty years ago," he said, hardly out of breath.

"And torture was big five hundred years ago. So what? When are you going to get your hair cut? Is that too difficult a question for you to answer? What do you have to say? Tomorrow? Next week? Next year? Never?"

I think he was squinting at me. "Hey, take it easy," he drawled.

"Sorry," I mumbled. "I have things on my mind."

Wally is my best friend. We have been in the same class since grade one. During our school career we've shared many things. It is our love of bicycles, however, especially bike jumping, that has made us true comrades. We'll set up a jump anywhere. All we need is a piece of board and something to rest it on.

Kids in St. Albert rate their jumping skill in terms of garbage cans. We put a garbage can on its side, make a ramp in front of it, take our bike fifteen or twenty metres away and pedal like you know what.

The idea, of course, is to jump over the can and land without wiping out. The trick is to know how to shift your weight the instant the front wheel leaves the ramp so the bike remains fairly straight in the air so when you land the front wheel doesn't turn and throw you off.

If you're a one-canner it means you've cleared and survived a garbage can. The first can is a big plateau. It isn't easy working up the courage to ride your bike in midair.

If you can hurl over two cans side by side you're a two-canner. Only a few reach this stage. A three-canner is a rare person. A true expert.

A four-canner is a pro, one of the gifted. Hardly anybody tries, let alone clears, four garbage cans. I've seen some people really get hurt trying four cans.

Wally and I are the only kids in town who have jumped five and lived to tell the tale, so to speak. I'm not trying to brag by saying that. It's just that we have a natural instinct for it. Wayne Gretzky is a born hockey player and Wally Stutzgummer and I are natural bike jumpers.

Neither of us had managed to clear six cans yet. I had a wrecked wrist to remind me of my failure, and Wally had a slightly crooked nose.

"So you're going to Toronto then?" he said.

"I didn't say that," I protested.

"You didn't say you weren't. That means you are."

Wally knew me too well. "It doesn't mean that at all."

He nodded, making his hair bounce up and down.

"I'm just thinking, that's all," I told him.

"Thinking about being Ms Teeny-Wonderful?"

"No way!" I shouted. I told him about the prizes,

especially the five thousand dollars.

"That would be nice."

"Sure would," I insisted. "Think of it. I could buy that Honda 250 Trail." I paused, gathering my thoughts. "It scares me, Wally. I don't want to be Ms Teeny-Wonderful, but I do want the prizes. Is that wrong?"

"What do you think?" he asked.

"I think that the end is worth the hassle, Wal. I think that all the stuff I'm going to have to put up with is worth the end. Think of how great it will be jumping on my motorbike."

"What if you don't win?" Wally said soberly.

His question caught me by surprise. Until that point I hadn't thought of the fact that I would probably lose. There were forty-nine other Teeny-Wonderfuls entered in the contest, and no doubt at least forty-eight of them were going to be more prepared for it than I was. The chance of winning was slim.

But it was a chance. I had one chance in fifty of winning that five thousand. If I didn't enter, I wouldn't have any chance at all.

"I'm going to do it," I announced. The words came out of my mouth with more conviction than they held in my mind. Wally's face mirrored the doubts I could still feel inside.

Carol Weatherspoon, I thought, do you realize

that you are selling yourself out for a chance at a few dollars? Do you understand that you are about to become a contestant in something as vulgar as a Ms Teeny-Wonderful contest? I felt a wave of nausea pass through me. Carol, this just isn't you.

3
Five-canners don't go on dates

When I arrived home the smell of frying lamb chops teased my nostrils. "Hi, Mom," I said, walking into the kitchen. I noticed a special delivery manila envelope on the table. It was addressed to me and had the *Canada Woman* logo on one corner. The package had already been opened.

"What's this?" I asked.

Mother was humming as she mixed up mint sauce. "Oh, that's all the information for the Ms Teeny-Wonderful contest. It has our airline tickets and our hotel confirmation. It also tells how the contest is going to be judged."

"Shall I read it through or will you tell me all about it?" I said sarcastically with a glance at the torn envelope.

Mother didn't miss a breath. "The whole contest will take three days, although when it goes on TV it will be edited down to one hour. The first evening there will be a big welcoming supper where you'll meet the editors of *Canada Woman.* The next day each girl will have an interview with the editors, and that night there will be a dance."

"A dance? What kind of dance?"

Mother ignored my question. "The third day there will be a visit to a museum in the morning, and in the afternoon the Parade of Charm. That's when all the contestants will parade before the judges in their fancy clothes. Following that the judges will choose five grand finalists. Those five girls will perform their talents and whoever makes the best impression will be crowned Ms Teeny-Wonderful."

Sounds fairly straightforward, I thought.

"Have you decided to go, dear?" Mother asked.

"I'm still thinking about it," I said. No need to tell her that I had already made up my mind. Best to keep her hanging and let her butter me up some more.

I flipped casually through the material in the envelope. It was as Mom had described, but I noticed that there were *three* airline tickets.

"Who's the other ticket for?" I questioned.

"For your escort, if you want to bring one," Mom replied.

"An escort? What's that?"

"A boy, dear," she smiled. "The *Canada Woman* people think it would be nice if you went to the dance and the museum with a boy. If you want to bring your own they will pay his fare and hotel room as well. If you don't, they say that they'll find one for you in Toronto."

"Go with a boy? That's a date!" I protested. "Mother, I only turned twelve last month. I'm too young to date. You and Dad told me I couldn't go out with boys until I was fourteen. I don't want to go on a date. Give me a break."

"Well, it's not really a date, is it?" Mom said as she tasted the mint sauce. "Needs more sugar."

"Sounds like it to me!" I shouted. "I don't want to go to a dance. I can't dance. You have to hold on to boys when you dance. I don't want to hold on to anybody, least of all a boy."

"You could ask Wally Stutzgummer to go with us," Mom suggested. "You seem to get along fine with Wally."

"Wally is my friend. We're five-canners together. I don't want him to be my date. It would spoil our friendship."

"Then we could let *Canada Woman* decide on an escort."

I thought about that for a millionth of a second. There was no way I was going to go to Toronto and spend my time with some jerk who would want to hold me and dance. I grew sick at the thought. At least Wally knew me. At least he wouldn't, and probably couldn't, dance.

"I'll ask Wally," I said.

Mother beamed. "Does that mean you've decided to go?"

"I'm still thinking about it," I said again, but Mother couldn't hear me. She was too busy singing some stupid song about it being a beautiful morning, even though it was six-thirty in the evening.

* * *

"What's an escort?" Wally asked me.

I gave the telephone receiver an angry look. I knew I should have biked over instead of calling him. "It's the person who accompanies me to some of the things," I repeated.

"What things?"

"The trip to the museum and stuff. Come on, it's a free trip to Toronto. Why are you so suspicious?"

"All I have to do is walk around with you?" he asked.

I nodded at the phone. "That isn't so bad, is it? We walk around together all the time."

"Yeah, but I don't walk around with you as an escort. An escort sounds like a fancy word for a date," Wally grunted.

"Well, it isn't!" I exploded. "Get real, Wally. Would I ask you to be my date? Do five-canners go on dates? I'm doing you a favour. I'm offering you a free trip across Canada, and you're complaining because you think I'm asking you on a date. Do you know what you are, Wally? You're—"

"Okay, okay. No need to get nasty. I'll go with you and be your escort on one condition."

"No way," I blurted. "No conditions. Either you want to come because you're my friend and I want you there, or we forget it."

"You want me there?" he drawled.

I mumbled a positive reply. Having Wally with me would at least make the Ms Teeny-Wonderful thing more bearable.

"You want me to be there?" he repeated.

"Give it a rest. I said yes already."

"Okay, I think I'd like that. I'm sure my mom will say it's fine. She likes you, even though she thinks you're strange."

"Return the compliment," I told him. "By the way, what was your condition?"

"That you let me ride your trail bike," he said slowly.

"No way!"

* * *

I went to my room, thinking about how much my life had changed in the last few hours and how much it could change in the future if I won the contest.

The talent thing bothered me. I hated poetry. If I got as far as the grand finals, how was I going to recite a poem on national TV and pretend that I liked it?

Then I froze. My stomach did a little heave-ho

and sweat broke out on my upper lip. "Oh no," I moaned. "Oh no!"

Poetry? The winter poem?

"Oh no," I said again.

The winter poem! It wasn't mine. That stupid poem about the winter's morning wasn't mine! Mr. Robinson assigned a poem that described the feelings of a season. When I went home and opened my brother Henry's grade eleven English text, the first poem about seasons I came across was about a winter's morning. I copied it onto foolscap and handed it in. When I read it to the class I deliberately made mistakes so nobody would notice. I was so good at sabotaging the thing that everybody thought it was funny, except Mr. Robinson. He gave me an A and showed a copy to my mother on interview day.

The poem was probably famous, a classic. I had fooled Mr. Robinson and my mom, but there was no way I could fool a national TV audience. There must be thousands of people out there who would know I had cheated.

"Oh no," I moaned.

4
Can't we take the train?

The next two weeks sped by. I alternated in mood between extreme calmness and outright fear. The latter I hid very well.

I was petrified about being exposed as a poetic cheater. I frantically thought of excuses to tell the editors of *Canada Woman* when they unearthed my deceit. What would they believe? "I'm sorry, but I was insane when I submitted my language arts assignment," "Excuse me, but this isn't my poem. I've been the victim of the dreaded poem-switcher," or "Isn't that a coincidence? I seem to have written a poem identical to What's-his-name's. Small world isn't it?" No matter how hard I tried, I couldn't get away from it — I was up that dirty creek without a paddle.

I tried to blank the poem thing out of my mind, hoping that I'd wake up in the morning and discover the problem had vanished. This brought temporary relief, but it also allowed me to think of my second fear.

I was petrified by the idea of flying.

That's right. I was scared to death of getting into an airplane. And I'd never even set foot near one.

This was no little fear. It was the big scaryoo! It's called a phobia. Lots of people suffer from phobias. Some are afraid of heights, others of closed-in spaces. My phobia, my utmost uncontrolled fear, was flying where there ought to be nothing but clouds.

So every time I pushed the poem thing to the back of my mind, the fear of flying thing came forward. I tried to talk it over with Wally the night before we left for Toronto.

"Wally, have you ever flown anywhere before?"

He nodded. "Sure, hasn't everybody?"

"Yeah," I said, trying to be casual. "Yeah, probably everybody in the world, except maybe a couple of babies who are too young."

"Sure." Wally nodded as if I was making sense.

"Does it scare you, Wally?" I asked.

"What?"

"Geez, are you thick today or what? Flying, does it scare you?" I said with frustration.

"Nope, why should it?"

Boy, sometimes I hate him! I could think of five hundred reasons why everyone should be scared of flying. I chose one that made the most sense to me. "Aren't you afraid that one of the wings is going to fall off?"

"Off what?"

"Save me!" I yelled. "What do you mean, off what? What else can wings fall off of? Off the plane!"

"Wings don't fall off planes," said Wally matter-of-factly.

"How do you know?" I challenged. "Are you an aviation engineer?"

Wally began to scratch his head. Obviously my chaotic questions were confusing him.

"I've never heard of a wing falling off a plane," he mumbled, unsure of how to proceed.

"Never?" I asked hopefully.

He shook his head slowly. "Never."

"Thanks, Wally," I said, feeling much better. I had never heard of it happening either, so if Wally hadn't, then maybe it didn't happen.

"Thanks for what?" he said.

"Oh nothing." I brushed his question aside, anxious to continue. "Wally, have you ever heard of an engine falling off a plane?"

"Ha, ha, ha." He began to laugh the same way he talks—slowly, as if each chuckle had to be divided into syllables.

"What are you laughing at?" I howled.

His chuckles diminished the way a radio does when the volume is slowly being turned down. "It wasn't supposed to be a joke?" he asked.

"Of course it wasn't supposed to be a joke! There's nothing funny about that."

"Guess not," he mumbled.

"I was trying to have a serious conversation," I said indignantly.

"Oh."

"Yeah, oh," I mimicked with sarcasm.

"Carol," Wally said, looking into my eyes as straight as he could with his still uncut hair, "Carol, are you afraid of flying?"

"Of course not," I lied. "What would give you such a stupid idea?"

"Guess I'm just reading between your questions," he said.

"Don't," I threatened. "Because you're wrong. Flying doesn't scare me at all."

"It's okay to admit you're scared, you know. I'm scared of things too," my five-canner buddy confessed.

"Like what?" I asked curiously.

He began to scratch his head again. "Well, I'm really afraid of gila monsters."

"Of what?" I said.

"Of gila monsters. Yeah, gila monsters really scare me."

"What in heaven's name is a gila monster?"

"It's a large lizard that lives in the desert regions of the southern United States and Mexico."

"Wally, we live over fifteen hundred kilometres from the nearest desert."

"Yeah," he nodded. "Good job too. If we lived any closer I'd be worrying all the time."

"Good night, Wally," I announced. "We'll pick you up at seven tomorrow morning. The plane leaves at nine."

* * *

The next morning we got up early. At least, those of us who hadn't been up regularly every half hour all night long got up early.

We had breakfast, then threw the last few things into our suitcases. I had been packed for almost a week. Actually Mom had done most of the work. She had been just beaming through the last two weeks. She had enough excitement about the Teeny-Wonderful thing for both of us.

I had been a good little Teeny-Wonderful for her. We'd gone out shopping several times, looking for the best dress-up dress in Edmonton. After trying on what seemed like a hundred, we had chosen three, all long, dressy and expensive. We spent a great deal of time finding the one I'd wear during the Parade of Charm. When we finally chose it, even I believed I had an outfit that would wow them.

We had also visited a hairdresser, where I'd had my hair permed in loose waves. I usually wore it straight down and did nothing with it except wash it twice a week, if I remembered. After the hairdresser had finished with it my mom *oohed* and *aahed* for about fifteen minutes. I didn't think it was bad either.

I had even let Mom experiment with putting a little bit of make-up on me: eyeshadow, pale lipstick, a little blush. The contest info said that make-up was allowed, as long as it wasn't overdone. I don't like cosmetics. Even with the modest amount Mom applied, I thought I resembled a hideous creature from a 3-D horror movie. Mom flattered me by telling me what a young lady I looked like. That turned me off even more. I only very reluctantly agreed to allow a small bit of make-up when the time came.

So I was set to travel across the continent and enter the Ms Teeny-Wonderful contest. While I was brushing my teeth before packing my toothbrush, I wondered about the people at *Canada Woman* who had thought up the name.

According to the contest literature the name was supposed to represent girls who were just on the verge of becoming teenagers. I thought that it sounded like a miniature hot dog or a doll that wets and barfs on itself. But they were no doubt smarter than me. Besides, it was their contest and their five thousand dollars.

As I closed my suitcase, my mind returned to the plane trip and my stomach rolled over. I'll never be able to do it, I thought. I'll never be able to get on the plane.

"Mom," I called, "can we take the train?"

She was putting on her jacket. "The train?" she

said. "Whatever gives you such funny thoughts? Get your bag and let's go. We have to pick up Wally."

The Edmonton airport is about twenty kilometres outside the city, a good hour's drive from St. Albert. That gave me plenty of time to get even more upset about getting into a huge vehicle made of steel that everyone expected to leave the ground. By the time we had arrived at the departure doors and Dad had unloaded our luggage I was in a sorry state, but Wally was the only person who noticed.

"Take it easy," he said.

I nodded dumbly.

"It's gonna be okay," he continued. "Engines don't fall off, you know."

That did it. "Oh sure," I snapped sarcastically, giving him a dagger glare. "Nothing ever happens to airplanes. Don't be so silly."

Dad hustled us into the check-in line where we waited for fifteen minutes, shoving our luggage slowly forward, until it was our turn to confirm our seats.

"Good morning," the attendant chirped. "How are we today?"

"All fine," my mother chirped back.

Speak for yourself, I thought.

"And where are we going?" The attendant smiled as she took our tickets.

"Toronto," Mother told her. "We're on our way to the Ms Teeny-Wonderful contest. My daughter is a finalist."

It was obvious that the attendant had never heard of the Ms Teeny-Wonderful thing and didn't want to now. She just nodded her head and said, "That's nice."

"She'll be on TV," Mom continued, ignoring her lack of interest.

"That's nice," the attendant replied in a monotone. "Will that be smoking or non-smoking?"

"Non-smoking, please," Mom answered. "The contest is being sponsored by *Canada Woman* magazine."

"That's nice. Please go to gate number seven. The plane will be boarding in approximately twenty minutes."

"Where's the pilot?" I demanded suddenly.

"Pardon me?" the woman answered.

"The pilot. Where's the pilot? I want to see the pilot."

"What on earth for?" asked my mother in a puzzled voice.

"I just want to say hello to the pilot." Actually I wanted to check him over, make sure that he wasn't drunk or hung over or blind or crazy or whatever.

"I imagine that the pilot is on the plane doing the pre-flight check. If you ask the steward or stewardess sometime during the trip, perhaps they will take you to the cockpit."

By then it will be too late, I thought darkly.

As we marched through the terminal, Wally

tried again to calm me down. "I read somewhere that flying in a plane is fourteen times safer than riding in a car," he said.

I didn't believe him. At that point I wouldn't have believed anything. The only thing I knew was that in half an hour I was going to commit suicide by climbing into a red and white airplane that was about to end its life in a fiery ball at the end of a runway.

At the entrance to waiting room seven we kissed and hugged Dad goodbye. Even Wally kissed him, which gave Dad a kind of strange look and made him shake his head. I grinned in spite of myself. Good old Wally.

As we went through the door we were met by two smiling security guards. Does everyone smile at airports? One of them, the female, asked me to place my small purse on a conveyor belt that ran into a strange looking machine. The belt started and my handbag was sucked into the machine.

"This way, please," said the other guard. He directed me up a small ramp and through what looked like a doorway with no door. When I had passed through he said, "Thank you," and handed me my purse, which had appeared from the other side of the bag-eating machine. Then he waved Mother through the pretend doorway and gave her her bag.

Then it was Wally's turn. As he went through, a bell started ringing.

"One moment, please," said the male guard. He

picked up a wand and started passing it over Wally's clothing. As it passed his belt buckle, it made a humming noise. The guard waved it over the buckle a few more times, then said, "Thank you very much."

"What's all that about?" I asked Mom.

"Airport security," she said, which didn't tell me anything. It was Wally who filled me in on the details.

"The machine you put your purse through is an x-ray," he explained. "It lets them see inside your hand baggage. That door thing is a metal detector. It picks up large metal objects like my belt buckle."

"Why do they do all that?" I asked, feeling that I should know about this so I could get upset about it.

"Security," Mom said.

"Hijackers," Wally elaborated. "In case somebody is bringing a gun on board to make the pilot take the plane somewhere else. This stops them. Hijackings used to happen a lot a few years ago. Now they don't happen as often because it's harder to smuggle a weapon on board."

"Now that's a good thing," I proclaimed. "That is a smart move."

"It also stops most of the bombs," Wally continued.

"Bombs? What do you mean bombs? Why would anyone want to bring a bomb on a plane? You're joking, right?" I sputtered.

Wally shook his head. "Some people smuggle an

explosive onto a plane and then tell the airline that it's going to go off unless they pay a large sum of money. It happens a lot. It's called extortion."

"Hardly a lot," Mother said. "It happens occasionally."

Occasionally sounded like a lot to me, especially since I was about to get on a plane. Now I not only had to worry about the engines falling off, I also had to worry about some kook bringing a bomb on board and blowing us up. Thanks, Wally. Thanks a whole lot.

5
The Great Swamp Jump

We sat in the waiting room, Mom reading her romance, Wally reading the old Marvel edition of *The Return of the Jedi*, and me gnawing my knuckles and glancing around to see if I could spot any suspicious characters.

I was a jumble of nerves, a real mess. Every time Wally turned a page I jumped. Finally he noticed.

"Carol, have you really thought about it?" he asked, putting his battered comic down on his lap and smiling at me.

"Of course I have," I growled. "I'm thinking about it all the time. How can something that weighs that much get off the ground?"

He chuckled under his breath and I gritted my teeth. "Not about the plane. About the contest and the chance of winning. You could be the first ever Ms Teeny-Wonderful."

I nodded, still surveying the people in the lounge to see if anyone was acting suspicious. "Yeah, I've thought about it a little," I admitted. "But I've had a couple of other things on my mind too, so I guess I haven't *really* thought about it."

"You'll get to visit all over Canada," he told me. "And probably all over the States as well. You'll be flying someplace new every week."

I looked at him and let my mouth drop open. I *hadn't* thought of that. "Oh great," I moaned. "Nothing could make me happier."

"And around St. Albert," Wally rambled on, "you'll be a celebrity. All the kids will want your autograph. Even Krazy Kurt'll probably talk to you. He may even ask you out."

"What are you talking about?"

"Well"—Wally rubbed the side of his nose with his finger —"you know how Krazy Kurt likes to be the first to get something nobody else has. Remember, he was the first kid to get a BMX. He was the first to get a Walkman. He was the first to make his dad buy him one of those talking computers."

"So?"

"So he is going to want to be the first guy to take you out. Face it, Carol, if you are picked as Ms Teeny-Wonderful, the most charming and talented girl in Canada, then all kinds of guys are going to want to be your boyfriend. Krazy Kurt is going to want you as his girlfriend more than anything."

"You're nuts," I protested. "Kurt isn't going to want anything to do with me. Not ever. He hasn't even spoken to me since the Great Swamp Jump."

Wally's smile almost split his face in two. The Great Swamp Jump had been one of my jumping buddy's greatest moments.

* * *

It had happened early last May. Krazy Kurt had just got a brand-new Redline. It was a beautiful trick bike with a beautiful sticker price. What K.K. wanted, he got.

I still had my old Raleigh at that time, and Kurt was always driving around telling me in impolite terms what a piece of garbage I was pedalling. Kurt was doing the same to Wally too, except that Wally wasn't as outspoken. He took things in his quiet manner and merely looked at Kurt as if he wasn't worth bothering about.

With his new bike the double K was building up a good rep as a jumper. He could clear three cans without a problem, and tried for four. To my chagrin he made it, and he did it looking good all the way. It was a perfect leap.

At that time Wally was the only other kid in town who had cleared four cans. It was natural for things to boil down to a big showdown between the two.

One day Wally and I were trailing through the field behind the school when Krazy Kurt rode up with five of his buddies.

"Hey, Wallabee," he shouted, "I wanna talk to ya." He pedalled up beside my buddy and stopped.

"Hey, ugly," he said to me.

"Afternoon, porkface," I smiled.

He gave me a dirty look and spat out an equally dirty word.

"Try it first and tell me about it," I shot back.

"Cool it," Wally said to me. "What do you want, Kurt?" he asked.

"I want a race," Kurt grunted. "You and me. See who's best. Or maybe a jump-off. Try for five cans. Whadaya say, Wallabee? You got the guts to try me?"

Wally looked at Kurt through his growing bangs. Then he looked at me and the rest of the guys. "Course I've got the guts," he said quietly. "That's never in question. Whether I have the skill may be another thing. So let's find out."

There were a few shouts of approval from the crowd.

"Let's make it a jump-off," Wally suggested. "Only not with garbage cans. Let's jump for distance, okay?"

"Yeah, sure thing, Wallabee," Krazy Kurt agreed. "Let's do it."

Wally pointed to the far end of the field. "Just down by the creek there, is a patch of muskeg. On the other side of the bog is sand. I was looking down there today and there's a sharp rise just before the swamp.

We can go down the hill, take off over the rise, clear the muskeg and land in the sand. The tires will leave their mark in the sand so we can see who jumped the farthest."

"Sounds good," Krazy Kurt nodded.

I looked at Wally suspiciously. Something was up.

When we biked over to the hill it was just as Wally had described. There was hard-packed river sand near the creek and a small patch of bog at the bottom of the slope. Directly in front of the bog was the mound that Wally proposed as the take-off ramp.

I studied the pile of grass-covered earth. Something about it wasn't right. At first glance it appeared fine, but there was something wrong.

"Wally," I said quickly, "can I talk to you alone?"

Some of the guys hooted and I made a rude gesture to them. I didn't like being nasty, but sometimes you've got to let people know you're not going to take any you know what.

Wally pulled in beside me. "What's up?"

"You can't jump down there," I told him. "The angle of that mound is too steep. You scoot down the hill and hit that and you'll just go right up in the air. You won't get any distance."

"I know that," he said slowly. "That's why I came here."

"What are you—"

"Come on, Wallabee!" Krazy Kurt hollered, interrupting me. "Stop flirting with your girlfriend."

Wally pedalled over to the group. "You want to go first?" he asked the double K.

Kurt looked down the hill. "Naw," he said, "you go."

Wally pushed on his pedals and directed his bike down the hill. About halfway down he swung out to the left and then turned to the right, so that he was approaching the mound at an angle.

"What's he doing that for?" Kurt grunted. "He ain't gonna get a whole lot of distance coming in on that thing sideways. What a jerk!"

Kurt was right. The bike hit the rise and sailed slowly over the top. Wally pulled at the handlebars, trying to get some distance, but his BMX barely carried him over the bog.

Kurt started laughing like a hyena. The other guys joined in. "Hey, Wallabee," he shouted, "my little baby sister can do better than that." He turned to me. "What a nothing your boyfriend is," he taunted.

"Your turn, mooseface," I smiled.

He gave me a dirty look again. "You're gonna see some class now," he told me.

I just shrugged at him and watched Wally skirt the swamp and push his bike up the hill.

"You didn't have no speed, Stutzgummer," Kurt admonished. He stood up on his pedals and drove about twenty metres into the field before stopping and turning. "Stay outta my way," he yelled. "I'll be going faster than the speed of fright."

We all backed away from the brink of the hill. K.K. began charging toward us. His head was down and I could see the veins on his forehead as he pushed violently at his pedals. As he built up speed, he began to scream. It was a mad holler, full of blind energy.

"What a sound," I said to Wally.

"Look at him move," Wally mumbled.

Kurt was hurtling across the short grass, still screaming, teeth showing. Instinctively we all backed farther away from the edge. I had a vision of a bull charging head first into the bull-ring boards.

"Maybe we should tell him," I said.

"Tell him what?" Wally asked innocently.

Kurt zoomed past us, leaving a noticeable breeze. His Redline leaped from the edge and flew through the air in a graceful arch before landing on the slope. As the tires landed, Kurt squealed louder and pedalled with increasing velocity for the take-off mound.

"I can't look," I whispered.

But I did. Kurt hit the pile dead on. The bike moved up the small bump quickly. In fact, it was a little too quickly.

"Holy—" somebody muttered.

It was just as I had foreseen. At such a high speed, the angle of that mound of dirt sent the bicycle straight up instead of forward.

Kurt stopped screaming and we could all hear him yelling a string of swear words that I didn't think went together. His bicycle went at least two metres into the air. It seemed to hang there for a moment, suspended so that we could witness Kurt's failure. Someone beside me groaned as the bike and rider dropped to the ground again. There was a loud splash as his body smacked into the muskeg.

A respectable spray of dirty water exploded from the swamp as Kurt came to rest. One of his buddies rushed down the hill and helped him stagger to his feet. He was covered in the black, dead moss of the bog. We could almost smell him from the top of the slope.

Suddenly we all broke into laughter. Watching Krazy Kurt trying to send himself into orbit and then seeing him soaked with putrid bog water was an experience that would be retold around the school for weeks to come.

"Always thought you'd make a good astronaut," one of his friends called down.

"Hey, now can I take a ride on the Kurt Shuttle?" said another.

"This ain't the time to take a bath, Kurt," yelled a third.

And so it went. I would have added my bit about anybody seeing an unidentified flying BMX, but I was laughing too hard.

* * *

My mother was tugging at my sleeve. I tried to stop laughing and wiped my eyes. "Oh, Wally," I said. "That was truly one of your greatest moments."

He was smiling and nodding. "Yeah, yeah," he said.

Mom pulled at my sleeve again. "Come on, you two, we're boarding the airplane now."

I choked on what laughter was left as my present situation returned to my mind. I looked at Wally. "Thanks," I said quietly. "You helped me forget for a couple of minutes. I needed to do that."

"I know," Wally said. "Let's go to Toronto, okay?"

"Okay," I smiled.

6
Are we there yet?

Mom sat in the seat next to the window. I had insisted. Wally sat in the seat across the aisle from me. I tried to make casual conversation by observing that the seats were more roomy than I had thought they would be. Wally glanced up from the folder he was studying and informed me that this was a Boeing 767, the newest and most advanced plane ever to fly. The only thing that told me was that the thing hadn't been tested long enough. I was being used as a guinea pig for the airlines. So much for casual conversation.

"I have to go to the bathroom," I said to my mother.

Mom pointed to the seatbelt sign. "Wait until the plane takes off, then you can go."

"I can't wait that long," I said. "I have to go to the toilet now."

She gave an exasperated sigh. "You're a big girl. Wait."

"But my stomach aches. I have this awful pain in

my gut," I pleaded.

She gave me a parental look of concern and put her hand on my forehead. "You're not warm," she observed, then reached down to feel my stomach.

A thin smile crossed her lips. "Here's the problem," she said as she released my seatbelt. The discomfort that stretched across my abdomen was instantly relieved. "No wonder you have a stomach ache. Your seatbelt was too tight."

I had tightened it as hard as I could on purpose. When the plane crashed I wanted every chance I could get.

As I refastened it, fractionally looser, the flight attendant began a little speech about safety exits and oxygen masks which didn't make me feel any safer. Then the 767 began to taxi down the runway.

I grabbed my armrests so tightly that my knuckles turned white.

"Relax," Wally said. "We have to get into position to take off first."

"We're not in the air yet?" I said through clenched teeth.

Wally shook his head.

The plane rolled to a stop. "What's wrong? Did the engines stall or something? Does that mean we won't be able to take off?" A note of hope crept into my voice.

"We're just waiting for clearance from the air traffic controllers. We can't take off if there's another plane landing, can we? We might hit it in midair."

"Oh great," I moaned. Something else to be disturbed about.

The engines gave a high-pitched roar and I was forced back in my seat. There was an overwhelming feeling of acceleration, of gaining speed.

"We're out of control!" I yelled.

Mother took my right hand. "What's the matter, dear?"

Wally was holding my left hand across the aisle. "We're just gaining speed so that we can take off."

His words were lost as the engines roared even more ferociously. The plane seemed to be hurtling down the runway at tremendous speed.

"We're doomed!" I screamed. "We're going to crash!"

The passengers sitting near us had turned to watch me go berserk. Most of them were smiling at me. I closed my eyes, ready for the metal-crunching smash as a forty million dollar airliner disintegrated and ended all our lives.

I waited for the inevitable, saying my prayers, reviewing my short, uneventful life. I had only just passed grade six. I hadn't done anything yet. I hadn't even jumped over six garbage cans.

"Okay," Wally said. "It's okay," he said again, squeezing my hand.

"Of course it's not okay," I yelled. "We're going to crash in a few seconds."

"No," he drawled. "We've taken off. We're in the air. We're flying."

I opened my right eye and looked around. The other passengers were reading newspapers or magazines. A couple of them had briefcases open, doing work. Everything was calm. No one was on fire or scrambling for an emergency exit.

I opened the other eye. "We're in the air?" I said cautiously.

"Yeah," Wally stated. "Look at the clouds outside your mom's window."

I decided to take his word for it.

"Are you all right?" I heard Mom asking.

I nodded. "No. I mean yes. I'm as good as can be, Mom, considering."

"I didn't know you were that excited over the Ms Teeny-Wonderful contest," she said.

I didn't even bother trying to explain the truth to her. Her head had been in the clouds long before we were airborne.

"How long is the flight?" I asked Wally weakly.

"Almost four hours," he said.

"A lifetime," I moaned.

* * *

We hit some turbulence over Lake Superior that made the plane bounce up and down a bit . Glancing out Mom's window I could see the old wing shaking. I had a slight fit. I figured a wing was only so much metal, and there was only so much rockin' and rollin' that metal could take.

Wally helped to calm me down. Later he persuaded me that the noise of the landing gear going down was not the bottom dropping off the airplane. By the time we landed, I felt too old for the Ms Teeny-Wonderful contest.

When the tires had touched ground and Wally had stopped me from cheering and waving my hands in the air, it was my mother's turn to become excited.

"Oh, this is really it," she giggled. Since the letter had arrived from *Canada Woman* she had been doing that a great deal. "We are really here. Really here in Toronto, and my precious baby is going to be in the Ms Teeny-Wonderful contest."

Precious baby, oh brother.

"Now you get ready," she said, running a brush through my hair and straightening the collar of my blouse. "There will probably be reporters and TV people waiting to take pictures when you get off the plane, so we have to look our best."

Somehow I doubted it, but I wasn't about to bring my mother down from such a pleasant mood.

We exited from the plane, and although I was disappointed that they wouldn't let me thank the pilot personally, I was happy to notice that there were no reporters or cameramen to greet me.

Mom was a trifle upset. "That doesn't seem

right," she said. "I would have thought that it would be good publicity to film the contestants arriving from all over Canada."

"With fifty contestants," Wally reasoned, "maybe it would have been a little redundant."

Mother nodded grudgingly.

"Redundant?" I asked Wally. "When did you start using words like redundant? If I recall, you were in the group that was reading *Jacob Two-Two* instead of *Mini-Bike Hero*."

"It's a new word I've learned," he explained. "Ever since school has been out I've been reading the dictionary and learning one new word a day."

"Oh," I said blankly, trying to picture Wally looking for a new word to learn.

We walked through the Toronto airport to the luggage pick-up area with the other passengers. I was feeling really good. I had survived a four hour plane flight. The angels were on my side. I could even think about the poem and figure that, just maybe, I could find a way out of my predicament.

The feeling lasted about half an hour. As we were taking a taxi to the Hotel Ontario I looked at the never-ending apartments, houses, factories, shopping malls, restaurants and hotels of Metropolitan Toronto. And everywhere people were buzzing around them.

It was seeing all those people that brought back

my anxiety about the poem. Seeing the population that made up national TV viewers made me realize how hopeless it was going to be to fool people with my copied poem. I could picture the scene in thousands of living rooms from Gander to Victoria:

"Hey, Martha, come and watch this kid on the Miss Teenage Weener thing."

"What is it, George?"

"Well, Martha, she's reciting this stupid poem on a winter's morning."

"So she is, George. Seems to me I've heard that poem before."

"By gosh, Martha, so have I. Dang me if that poem wasn't in my grade eleven textbook."

"Golly, George, you're right. That's that famous poem by What's-his-name."

"Well, I'll be a wounded prairie dog, Martha. That there Teeny-Wheezer is cheating."

"So she is, George. What a disgrace. Right here in front of the national TV audience."

"Disgusting, Martha. She should be tarred and feathered."

"Don't think so, George. Think she should be shot."

So many people. So large an audience. What was I going to do?

7
Double trouble

Our rooms in the Hotel Ontario had been reserved by *Canada Woman.* Mother and I shared a room with two double waterbeds and a fantastic view of the Toronto waterfront and the Island. Wally was placed in a room on the other side of the hallway with two single beds and a fairly decent view of the city. The desk clerk told him that he would have to share with another escort. Wally apparently didn't mind that, because he shook his hair in agreement.

On the desk in our room we found an invitation to the opening banquet for the Ms Teeny-Wonderful contest.

"We only have two hours to get ready," said Mom. "Perhaps we had better get started."

Usually I am a champion dresser. I can do it in less than a minute, with my eyes closed, at a quarter to nine. I am Bruno Walton's soulmate in this area. But on that afternoon it took me the whole two hours

Mom had threatened. By the time I had showered, washed my hair, dried it, styled it, dressed, allowed Mom to put on my modest amount of make-up and preened in front of the mirror for five minutes, it was time to go.

I could exaggerate and say that I thought I looked yucky and out of character, but that was only part of my feelings. Seeing myself all decked out made me feel curious about the strange alien being I had become. Even though I didn't really want to be the person that looked back at me in the mirror, I was still sort of pleased that underneath my regular appearance I could look fancy if I wanted to.

When we knocked on Wally's door he opened it and gasped. "Wow," he said. "Do you ever look sharp!"

"Thank you." I curtsied, enjoying just about the first nice thing I could remember Wally ever saying to me that didn't involve bike jumping.

"You too, Mrs. Weatherspoon," Wally added politely. "You also look very nice."

"Let me return the compliment, Wally. You're looking rather smart tonight as well," Mom said.

Wally grinned. "Yes, I do look sort of dapper, don't I?"

My escort was wearing a grey suit that was a little too small for him, but it did make him look good, considering that I'd only seen him wear jeans and a T-shirt before.

"Dapper?" I inquired.

"That's my word for today. It means smartly dressed," Wally explained.

We took the elevator down to the mezzanine level of the hotel and went to the doorway of the Simcoe Room. There we presented our invitation and entered the first function of the Ms Teeny-Wonderful contest.

A hostess checked off my name and directed Mom to a table on the perimeter of the room. Mom was a little upset about having to leave me, but the hostess insisted that it was the procedure for the evening. Finally Mom was convinced, and we watched her march away to join a table of other disgruntled mother-types.

Wally and I were escorted to one of the ten well spaced tables in the centre of the room. It was obvious that these tables were for the Ms Teeny-Wonderful contestants because every other place had an embossed place card with a girl's name on it. Mine read *Ms Carol Weatherspoon.* I thought the Ms was a nice touch. At the setting next to mine was a smaller card that said *Escort of Ms Weatherspoon.* Classy stuff.

In between my knife and fork was a pink carnation corsage, which didn't exactly go with my blue dress, but it was a nice gesture. At Wally's place was a single white carnation to stick in the buttonhole of his suit.

The table itself was set with silver and crystal.

The table linen was heavily starched, and a huge flower centrepiece finished the picture. I had to give it to *Canada Woman*. They sure knew how to put on an impressive spread.

In front of the contestants' tables was a long head table. A large banner with the *Canada Woman* logo was hung on the wall behind it. Obviously that was where the VIPs would sit.

There were two couples already at our table when we arrived. One of the girls was Shirley, from Moose Jaw, and the other was Dorothy, from Toronto. I've forgotten their last names, as I've forgotten the names of the boys they were with.

We made small talk for a few minutes, mostly complaining about our mothers and how we had been coerced into the contest. I tried to start a conversation about bike jumping, but it got nowhere. Only Wally was willing to talk about it.

The last four places at out table remained vacant until about one minute before the head table-party arrived. Then we were joined by two of the most beautiful girls I had ever seen, and their escorts.

Both girls were tall and blonde. Their hair was done perfectly and their matching dresses looked as if they had been made by a fashion designer. (I later found out that this was the case.) I looked at their faces to see how much of their good looks was make-up. At first I thought they weren't wearing any. I had to look really close before I could tell they were. It was so expertly put on that it looked as if a professional artist had done it. (I later found this to be the case as well.)

They were gorgeous. If this Teeny-Wonderful thing was going to be based on appearance alone, these girls were bound to be co-winners. It would have been impossible to choose between them. They were identical twins.

I glanced at their place cards. *Jean Louise Campbell* and *Joan Margaret-Elizabeth Campbell.* Their mother had entered both of them and they had both been selected as finalists. In fact, *Canada Woman* had allowed them to be considered as one contestant.

Even their escorts seemed too good to be real. They were older than most of the boys there, about fifteen. And they were both wearing what appeared to be tailor-made three-piece suits. (Guess what I found out later?)

The foursome sat down, gave everybody else a quick, haughty once-over, and then turned their attention to the head table, where those responsible for the contest were making an entrance.

There were six people in the head-table party: a representative from the City of Toronto, two adjudicators who had helped to choose the fifty finalists from the mailed-in entries, a representative from the airline that was presenting the prize trip to Disney

World, and two *Canada Woman* editors. It was on the last two individuals that most of the fifty contestants were focusing their attention. The other forty-nine were no doubt wondering, like me, what it would take to impress those two, who would be interviewing us tomorrow.

The Editor-in-Chief of *Canada Woman* was Irene White, a lady who was well known throughout the country. Before landing the job as boss of Canada's largest women's magazine she had been a TV news anchorwoman. She had even served one term as a Member of Parliament.

In appearance she seemed a severe woman, with tied-back brown hair, little make-up and a business suit. She seldom smiled. Her eyes, however, were soft and tender. As she surveyed the Ms Teeny-Wonderful finalists and her gaze rested on me, I felt an intense liking for her. I had a feeling that I could be friendly with that woman.

The other person who commanded our attention was the Promotion Editor, Henry Chaple. He was in charge of the Ms Teeny-Wonderful thing and had organized all the final functions. Unlike Ms White, he was always grinning, yet the smile seemed to be as silly as the ruffled shirt and tight jeans that he wore. He might be a very talented person, but his appearance didn't impress me very much.

After the head-table party was seated and the

rep from the city had welcomed us and wished us luck, they began serving the appetizer. It was a fresh fruit salad that contained mangoes and kiwis and whatever. I gave mine to Wally and watched him gorf it down.

As I buttered a bun I noticed the beautiful twins watching me. My initial reaction was to say something like, "You wanna stare, turn on a TV." But I didn't. I knew that if I was going to win my trail bike, then I had better start being the perfect Ms Teeny-Wonderful right now. There was no telling who was watching.

"Hi there," I said. "I like your hair and dresses. You look real nice."

I expected them to return the compliment, the way people do when they're making small talk. But they didn't do or say anything. They just kept looking at me.

"What's the matter? Do I have butter on my nose?" I joked.

The Jean twin leaned over to the Joan twin and whispered in her ear. That bugs me, when people whisper. I could feel the back of my neck getting hot.

"Are you two sisters?" Wally asked.

The stupid question helped cool me off. I wasn't sure if Wally was serious or not. Sometimes he says silly things to other people to get them going.

It was Joan's turn to whisper to Jean.

"It's impolite to have clandestine conversations," Wally said.

I looked at him. "New word?" I asked.

He nodded.

Joan raised her eyebrows and addressed my escort. "Our conversation is not secret," she said in the kind of diction that you save for your public speaking assignment. "And we weren't being impolite. Since what we were saying would have hurt your feelings, we politely kept it to ourselves." Her words were accompanied by a look of purest innocence.

"What were you saying?" I challenged.

"Merely that it is surprising what managed to pass the preliminary judging of the contest," said Jean with the same blandly innocent look as her sister.

"What managed to pass?" I repeated, knowing that I had been politely insulted.

"Yes," said Joan. "Take your case, for instance. Obviously the picture of you must have been most flattering."

I didn't care if they were nicely put insults or not. They were still insults. I gave the twins my evil eye.

I could feel Wally's hand tapping my knee. "Calm down," he said. "They're not worth it."

I looked at Joan's escort, who was grinning at me and nodding as if they'd just beaten me in something. I could feel my neck getting hot again. At that moment Irene White rose and took the microphone. Her deep, authoritative voice made me control my retaliation.

"Before you start your dinner," she began, "I want to welcome the fifty contestants, as a group, to the Ms Teeny-Wonderful contest sponsored by *Canada Woman* magazine. I hope you'll take this time to get to know one another. This is a competition in name only, and I want us all to be friends whether we win or lose.

"*Canada Woman* has not sponsored this contest in order to pick the most beautiful or the most talented girl in Canada. We do not want a winner in the contest any more than we want a loser. What we want to choose is a representative. We want a girl who stands for the modern Canadian pre-teenager. We want a girl who can succeed in what she chooses because of her skills and her personality.

"We want a representative to tour Canada for our magazine and say, 'Look, Canada. I am a Canadian girl. I can do this now, and I will be able to take up the challenge of the future.' We want someone to represent all the other ten- to thirteen-year-old girls across this nation."

There was a smattering of applause from around the room. My own opinion of the contest had risen as Ms White talked. Her description of it certainly made it sound different from the traditional beauty contest my mother had described when she first told me about it. I had reluctantly agreed to take part in Mother's contest in hopes of winning the prizes. This contest sounded easier to stomach.

Irene White was continuing to talk. "Tomorrow Mr. Chaple and I will be meeting with each of the fifty contestants. Although the interviews will be short, the impression you make on us will go a long way in determining our five grand finalists. In spite of this, I want you to be assured that we are looking forward to meeting you all.

"In the meantime, I hope that every one of you will enjoy your dinner and your evening here tonight."

There was more polite applause.

8
Hooligan!

After Irene White had seated herself again, dinner was served. It was pretty good—veal cutlet with melted cheese and ham in the middle. It was my turn to gorf. I spent time talking to Shirley and Dorothy, but avoided the Campbell twins. My anger was still simmering. I thought that if I could ignore them, then I could let their insults pass.

Henry Chaple made a speech before dessert telling everyone of the thousands of letters that *Canada Woman* had received for the Ms Teeny-Wonderful contest, the difficulty of arriving at fifty finalists and how we should all be so proud of ourselves.

We bore his speech politely and dug into our peach melba.

"So you say you come from St. Albert, Alberta?" It was Joan addressing me.

Perhaps she had decided to be friendly the way Ms White had suggested. I gave her the benefit of the doubt and nodded.

"How about you?" I asked.

"We're from Ottawa," they said in unison.

"I hear it's a nice place," Wally said.

"It's the capital city," said Jean. "You do know that, don't you?"

Again they were starting the belittling comments, delivering them with the most pleasant looks possible.

"Yeah, we know it," I said in a snarly tone.

"Tell me," said Joan, "what exactly is your talent? Looking at you, I wonder what you could possibly be skilled at."

I glared at her.

"Carol writes great poems," announced Wally.

"Writing poetry," said Jean. "That's kind of boring, isn't it? I mean, only dull people write poetry nowadays."

"Or slow people," Joan added.

Their escorts were smirking a little, enjoying the rudeness of their companions.

I grinned through clenched teeth.

"What do you do?" asked Wally.

"Oh, we play the concert piano," boasted Joan.

"We've won lots of awards," bragged Jean.

"But we never write poetry," Joan asserted, as if it was equal to sitting in dirty cat litter.

"I guess you must be pretty competent." Wally said. Then he turned to me and added, "New word."

"Where did you get your dress?" Joan asked.

"I don't remember," I said, my teeth still clenched. "Someplace in Edmonton."

"Must have been one of those discount stores," Jean observed.

"Probably on the clearance rack," noted Joan. "It's terribly out of style."

I put down my dessert fork. "Okay, you two turkey brains," I said. "I don't know what your stupid game is, but unless you knock it off you're going to be wearing your noses behind your left ears."

The twins and their escorts began to chuckle.

I turned to face Wally. "I'm gonna kill them, Wal," I said. "I'm gonna rip off their faces."

Wally grabbed me by the arm. "Don't do anything foolish," he said. "Float with it."

"Do all people in St. Albert talk that way?" Joan asked. "Or just the ones who are slightly disturbed?"

I started to push myself out of my seat, my fists tight. Again Wally's strong arms stopped me. Even behind his long bangs I could tell that he had a determined look.

"Now cool it," he said.

I kept my fists in tight balls, ready to pummel their stupid faces.

"Carol," he leaned over and whispered forcefully into my ear, "they are doing it on purpose. Can't you see that? They are trying to get you so riled up that you'll do something stupid."

I turned my head toward him so quickly that it hurt my neck. "You don't think I should punch them out?"

"They want to win the contest," Wally whispered. "If they succeed in getting you to look like a jerk in front of the editors, then there is one less person to worry about."

I took three deep breaths, trying to settle down. It wasn't easy. I'm not the type of person to let someone else give me a hard time. But Wally's logic seemed reasonable. He knew me, and so far what he had said since we started out had helped me.

"Okay," I nodded. "Okay, I'll stay cool."

"They have pills for people with your problem," Joan started again.

"When this is over, I'm going to come to Ottawa and bite off your ears," I smiled, controlling myself very well.

Our waiter came around asking if anyone would like coffee or tea. I looked at the editors to see if they were watching us. I know some adults don't think kids should drink either of those beverages. But neither one of them was paying any attention. I decided that Irene White couldn't have cared less anyway, so I ordered a coffee, which I like because it tastes so bad that it tastes good.

By the time the beverages were served, the atmosphere at our table had become pretty heavy. The twins talked quietly to their escorts. Shirley and Dorothy still made small talk with each other. But I just sat brooding and dreaming up new ways to get my revenge after the contest.

Television cameras appeared at the same time as the coffee and tea. A television reporter I recognized from the late news wandered among the contestants' tables, followed by a cameraperson. The reporter stopped and made small talk with the finalists.

The conversations were being recorded so that bits and pieces could be included in the final hour-long TV presentation of the contest. The rest of the events scheduled for the contest would be similarly prerecorded.

We all watched the reporter as she did her rounds, which was unfortunate for me. I should have been watching the twins and their escorts and what they were doing to my coffee.

She arrived at our table, asked Dorothy a few questions, then asked Shirley where she was from and how she was enjoying Toronto. "Too hot and too many people," was Shirley's reply.

The reporter turned to the twins in search of more promising material. She spent what I considered far too much time flattering them on the fact that they were both talented enough to be named as finalists and that *Canada Woman* had allowed them to be named as one entry. She then went on to point out that if Jean and Joan won, Canada would be receiving two Teeny-Wonderfuls for the price of one. It was so cute it made me want to throw up.

When she had finished with the twins she moved around toward me. I felt a flash of nervousness in my lower stomach and my mouth became dry. I reached for my coffee and took a large swallow before I had to talk.

I nearly gagged and spit the lukewarm coffee all over the national TV audience. My entire mouth was on fire. There was an overwhelming sensation of pain across my tongue and the inside of my cheeks. My eyes began to water. One of the twins or one of their boyfriends had dumped the contents of the pepper shaker into my coffee.

"Hello," said the reporter as she read my embossed place card. "This is Carol, and Carol is from...?"

My eyes were bulging. I swallowed the fiery liquid and let out a muted groan. I was instantly hit by a wave of nausea and my body began to sweat. When I opened my mouth to answer, I felt the heat surround my throat. "Ssaaghhh," I gasped, trying to make the words St. Albert.

"Pardon?" the reporter smiled.

"Ttt bbbberrrrr," I tried again. The process of talking was agonizing. I glanced at the twins and saw that their faces still showed the same perfect innocence. But I knew by the glitter in their eyes how hard they were laughing inside.

"And how do you feel about being in Toronto for this contest, Carol?" the reporter continued.

I looked at her through my tearful eyes, then I glanced back at the Campbell sisters. How dare they do this to me? Wally had his hand on my arm again, but he wasn't going to hold me back this time. I leaped from my seat and went flying with both arms outstretched into the amazed faces of my tormentors. I hit them with a wonderful thud that drove all three of us to the floor.

The unfortunate part was that I didn't have time to pummel them before their escorts and Wally pulled me off. My mother and the twins' mother were at the scene immediately.

"Carol, what on earth—?" my mom was squawking.

"Animal!" the twins' mother was yelling. "Hooligan! Animal!"

I saw myself on the news later. I looked like a crazy person. My eyes were bulging from the pepper and the anger. My face was red. Wally held my arms behind me, but I was struggling madly against his hold. In my pepper-induced fury I was shouting threats at the twins, who were slowly getting to their feet with hurt, bewildered looks on the faces they turned to the camera. But the only sounds coming out of my mouth were grunts and howls.

From the angle of the camera, you could see the head table behind me. Both Irene White and Henry Chaple were looking down on me with disapproving, disgusted stares.

9
The Pit

"I don't believe it," my mother said as she turned off the TV in our hotel room. "I just don't understand what came over my little girl."

"I told you, Mother," I repeated for at least the twentieth time. "Those twins put pepper in my coffee. They had been bugging me all evening."

"But to act so, so—" Mom was at a loss for words.

"Demented," Wally interjected. "She was acting demented."

"Enough with the new words," I shouted at him. "Mom, I *couldn't* let them get away with what they were doing."

"Fine," Mother scolded. "Just fine. And what did you achieve, Carol Weatherspoon? You made an utter fool of yourself in front of national TV and the editors of *Canada Woman*. Do you think they are going to choose someone who hurls herself across a table to punch fellow contestants as Ms Teeny-Wonderful? Oh, the embarrassment, the shame of it!"

"Mom," I pleaded, "it was your idea for me to enter this thing. What went on tonight was me. I told you I wasn't the Teeny-Wonderful type."

"That's right," Wally added. "Carol was certainly being herself this evening."

Mother began to sob.

Wally got off his chair. "I'm going to bed," he announced. "I'll see everybody at breakfast."

"Good night," I said. "Say hello to your new roommate for me."

"The Pit?" he grinned. "Sure."

Wally's fellow-escort had accompanied a girl called Lucy from Yellowknife. Wally had quickly nicknamed him the Pit because he was always eating. The Pit wasn't fat. In fact, he was on the skinny side, but his pockets were always stuffed with what seemed a never-ending supply of cupcakes and chocolate bars.

When my friend had left I turned again to Mother. "Mom," I reasoned, "I'll explain what happened to the editors tomorrow. They'll understand."

She just continued to wail. It's hopeless to talk to her when she's in that kind of mood, so I didn't try any more. I undressed quickly and got under the covers.

No matter how hard Mom cried, I didn't feel guilty about what I had done. If I hadn't retaliated I would have seemed a real jerk anyway, grunting and groaning into the TV camera. Besides, it would have let those turkeys think they could get away with their rudeness and messing around. And there was no way I was going to let them do that.

* * *

Things hadn't cooled down any in our room by the next morning. Mom woke up complaining of a headache and said she wanted to pass on breakfast. I could read the signs of a new bout of tears coming on, so I left quickly. I went across the hall to call on Wally. He was up, dressed in his more familiar jeans and T-shirt, lying on his bed watching *Gilligan's Island* on the TV.

There was a delicious smell of pancakes, sausage and bacon in the room. Wally's roommate, the Pit, was seated on the edge of his bed shovelling great mounds of food into his face from a tray on wheels.

"Have you already eaten?" I asked Wally, pointing to another tray with dirty breakfast dishes piled on it.

Wally shook his head. "Nope. That's the Pit's first breakfast. He's been calling room service."

I turned to the other boy. "May I ask you a personal question?" I said.

The Pit nodded, not missing a bite.

"Where do you put it all?"

He stopped and swallowed, washing the pancakes down with a huge gulp of milk. "Don't know.

I'm just hungry all the time."

"You sure are," I observed.

"The doctor says I've got something called inefficient metabolism, so I have to eat more than most people."

"I've heard of that," Wally said.

"Sounds like one of your new words," I noted.

"Gets kind of tricky at times," the Pit mumbled through link sausage. "I have to eat, but some foods take a long time to digest. Take onions, for instance. If I eat something with onions, then I can't eat again for another hour or so."

"Must be tough," I agreed.

He nodded. "Kind of puts pressure on the diaphragm. Makes it hard to sing."

"Sing or eat onions," I mused. "Tough choice."

"Kind of hard to run as well." The words were almost unintelligible through bacon and pancakes.

"Speaking of running and food"—I turned to Wally—"how about running to the restaurant?"

"How's your mom?" Wally asked as we left the room.

"Barely making it," I replied. "She says she has a headache. All I know is she's sure I've blown the Teeny-Wonderful contest."

"She may be right."

"Thanks for cheering me up," I grinned.

Wally returned the grin. "Boy, you should have seen the look on Joan and Jean's faces as you went flying across the table at them. If you did blow it, it was worth it."

We entered the restaurant, ordered bacon and eggs and sat watching the crowd. There were a few other girls our age. They probably belonged to the contest too, but I didn't recognize anybody. In our ordinary clothes we looked like different people.

"When's your interview?" Wally asked.

"Eleven forty-five. Then we're free for the day."

"Are you nervous?"

"No," I lied. "In fact, I'm looking forward to explaining why I decked those dopey twins last night."

"Maybe you shouldn't say anything about it."

"Why?" I asked, puzzled.

"Well, maybe they've forgotten about it. Or maybe they didn't realize it was you."

"Get serious," I laughed. "It's been on TV so many times that the *Canada Woman* people must be sweating staples. This is their big thing. Look how much money they've sunk into it. Their big chance at coast-to-coast publicity, and so far all they've got is one of their darlings punching out two others. They'll remember all right. They've probably carved my name in their desks."

The waitress brought our breakfast and stood staring at me for a few minutes. "Excuse me," she said, "aren't you the girl on the TV who beat up the other girls in that contest thing?"

I turned to Wally. "See what I mean?"

* * *

We ate a slow meal, then left the hotel for a short walk along the Toronto waterfront. I sure must hand it to the city. They've fixed it up so that people can walk along and enjoy themselves.

We stopped and looked at the skyline, impressed by the size of it all. The structure that dominates all others, of course, is the CN Tower, the tallest free-standing structure in the world.

Looking up at the thing made my neck hurt, but it was hard not to be impressed by all the concrete and work that went into it.

"Let's go up there this afternoon," Wally suggested.

"Are you serious?" I snorted. "You saw me in the plane. Do you want to see the same thing happen again? It will, you know. There's no way I'm getting into an elevator that goes up that high. I freeze in the hotel elevators. What if the cables broke when we were almost to the top? No way."

"I see your point," Wally said, "but these things are all pretty well a hundred percent safe, you know."

"It's the one-tenth of one percent that isn't safe that worries me," I told him.

"But just being alive has that much risk," Wally stated. "You've probably got more chance of being run over by a truck or drowning in the shower than of crashing in an elevator."

"Hardly," I scoffed.

"Just standing here is a risk," my friend drawled. "Just suppose a small meteor is entering the earth's atmosphere right now, burning up with the friction."

I scrunched up my face and looked at Wally, wondering what was going on beneath that long blond hair.

"And just suppose," he continued, "that the meteor is so big that it doesn't all burn up as it hurtles through the air. Suppose there's enough of it left to hit the ground, a piece the size of a softball—red-hot molten nickel from outer space."

"What the heck are you raving about?" I demanded.

"Risk," Wally said seriously. "The risk of being alive. Suppose this remnant of planetary garbage just happens to be heading for the same place where you are standing. Suppose you look up at the CN Tower at the very instant that it's due to land. As you glance skyward at a wonder of modern engineering, the meteorite runs into your face at five thousand kilometres an hour. Just suppose."

"Are you okay, Wal?" I asked quietly.

"Of course I'm okay. But you see, it all has risk, doesn't it?

"Uh-huh," I nodded, wondering how much sleep

Wally had had last night.

"So if you know that, then maybe you'll come up to the top of the tower this afternoon." He grinned as if he felt his logic would convince me it was sane to get into a little steel box and let mere cables lift and lower me to and from the ground.

"No way," I said.

He made his lips go thin, the way he does when he's starting to get angry. "Sometimes I don't understand you. You're the only other person I know who's tried to jump six garbage cans. You know what jumping over garbage cans is? It's stupid, that's what it is."

Wally was really getting worked up.

"You break bones," he emphasized. "You cut yourself. And there is a far greater chance of breaking your neck that way than there is riding in an elevator. You don't make any sense."

"Wally," I said, "in an elevator or a plane I have no control. None. If the cable snaps or the wings fall off there is nothing I can do about it. On my BMX I'm in control. If I do it all right then it works out. If I get scared or make the wrong move and I wipe out, then it's my fault. It isn't chance. Do you understand?"

"No," he said.

"A little?" I coaxed.

"Yeah," he said reluctantly. He looked at his watch. "We'd better get back. Your interview is in an hour and you probably want to get changed."

"Sure do," I said. "Wally?"

"Yeah?"

"Thanks for being my friend and saying you understand even when you don't."

"Yeah," he grumbled.

10
I want to be a cop, ma'am

Watching me change and get ready to meet the editors of *Canada Woman* did wonders for my mother's headache. I think she realized that the interview was a big part of the contest and that since Henry Chaple hadn't called to demand my immediate banishment, then maybe I still had a chance. Enough of a chance, anyway, for her to spend a little time trying to perfect the image I would present.

"Now remember, what are you going to call the editors?" she coached.

"Sir and ma'am," I said.

"And what are you always going to try to be?"

"A perfect little lady," I uttered sarcastically.

"Oh Carol," she pleaded, "you can do this. You can make me so proud."

Enough of the pressure stuff, I thought.

"Now," Mom continued, "remember all we talked about before we left. Don't tell them about the bicycle jumping. They certainly won't want a Ms Teeny-Wonderful who jumps over garbage cans. And if they ask you what you want to be when you grow up, say a doctor or a social worker, a job that helps other people."

"I want to be a cop."

"I know, dear," Mother said softly. "But we mustn't tell the editors that, must we?"

"Why not?" I asked. "Cops help people. What's wrong with being a cop?"

Mother sighed as if I was a frustrating toddler. "Because cops—I mean police—have a rather tough image. A Teeny-Wonderful shouldn't be too—how should I put it?—too strong."

"Doctors and social workers aren't strong?"

"Oh Carol!" she exhaled deeply. "You have to seem more feminine."

"I'm feminine," I said. "I'm your regular, average girl."

"Yes, dear, but sometimes you're not feminine enough."

"Oh," I teased. "Dad says that the girls in that magazine he reads with the foldout centre are really feminine."

"Carol Weatherspoon," she snapped, "stop giving me a hard time."

* * *

Mom and I took the elevator (reluctantly) to an

executive suite on the twenty-sixth floor of the hotel. Outside the door there was a large sign: *Ms Teeny-Wonderful Contestant Interviews. Please be seated. The editors will be with you shortly.* There were three large French Provincial style chairs in the hallway. Mom and I had barely sat down when the ornate door swung open.

Henry Chaple looked at us with a critical eye. He was wearing a flowered shirt and another pair of tight jeans. Perhaps he had a closet full of tight jeans.

"Carol Weatherspoon?" he said.

I nodded.

"That's my daughter, sir," Mom said. The molasses on her breath was almost real.

"Yes," Chaple grunted. "The flying girl. Come in, please."

Mother and I stood and walked toward the door, but Chaple held out his arm to bar Mom's way. "Sorry," he said, "we just interview the contestants. We find they are more honest without their mothers present."

Once again my mother looked hurt, but I felt that the arrangement was fine. I could certainly be more relaxed without her watching every move I made.

And I needed to relax. I could feel my knees going all shaky and the back of my throat constricting. I realized that this was important. Whether or not I had any chance of getting into the finals after what had happened last night would be determined in the next ten minutes or so.

As I stepped through the door I could see that the only other person in the room was Irene White. She sat on a sofa making notes on the top sheet of a pad of clipboard papers. Her hair was still tightly pulled back from her forehead and her tailored grey business suit made her look very threatening. Her eyes, however, still gave away the tenderness that was beneath the harsh exterior. She continued to work for half a minute before she acknowledged my presence.

Henry Chaple had seated himself in a large easy chair to the right of the sofa. I had remained standing, showing my manners. Ms White pointed to an armchair opposite the coffee table.

"Sit there, please, Carol," she said. She ripped the top sheet off her clipboard, and I saw her write my name on the top of the next page.

"I'll be blunt," said Henry Chaple. "After last night, I was ready to boot you back to St. Arthur."

"Albert," I corrected. "St. Albert, not St. Arthur."

"Whatever," Chaple waved his hand in frustration. "What you did last night didn't help the image of the Ms Teeny-Wonderful contest."

"Sorry, sir," I said in my nicest voice.

"What Henry is trying to say, Carol," Irene White explained, "is that we are attempting to run a contest with dignity here. Do you understand?"

"Yes, ma'am," I said.

"I want this contest to show the girls of Canada at their best. I don't want frilly, empty-headed little do-gooders. I want talented, vibrant, attractive and aware girls. Do you understand that as well?"

"Yes, ma'am," I nodded.

"But I do not want brawlers either. I abhor violence and I do not consider it a justifiable means of settling a dispute. Do you understand that?"

Abhor? What in heaven's name did abhor mean? Wally would probably know. "Yes, ma'am," I said again.

"And stop calling me ma'am, Carol. My name is Irene. Use it." She mumbled something about mothers under her breath. "Now," she continued, "what happened last night?"

I had been rehearsing what I was going to say since I got into bed last night. I was going to tell how the twins and their escorts had tried to sabotage my chances of being Ms Teeny-Wonderful, how I had merely retaliated against rudeness and plain ignorant behaviour. But now that I had my chance to speak, I changed my mind. No matter what I said, I knew that it wouldn't justify my actions in Irene White's mind.

"I lost my temper," I said. "I'm sorry."

"Sorry?" Henry Chaple scoffed. "Sorry is not good enough."

Ms White gave the Promotion Editor a quick glance, then stared at me. "You're telling us that nothing else happened, that you just tried to decapitate your fellow contestants?"

"Yes, Irene," I said, feeling awkward using her first name.

"The Campbell twins did nothing and said nothing to make you angry, to make you want to do them physical injury?" she continued to prod.

"No," I said. "Nothing that deserved what I did."

"Interesting," she said with a brief smile. "Perhaps after the contest you will tell me the truth about what happened." I had the feeling that I had said the right thing.

At a glance from Irene, Henry Chaple reluctantly offered me some apple juice, which I thankfully accepted to ease my dry throat.

"We have a few questions to ask you that all the other contestants are being asked as well," he said. "Please answer honestly."

"Shoot," I said.

"Pardon?" he inquired.

"Okay, ask away, sir," I told him.

He looked down at a paper on the coffee table. "Do you read *Canada Woman* magazine?"

What were they asking that for? Maybe they thought that if I read it I would be a better representative for them. "Sometimes," I answered, figuring that would be a safe response.

"Sometimes?" Chaple raised his eyebrows.

"Well, some of the stuff."

"Some of the stuff?" said Irene White. "Like what stuff?"

I decided to be honest. "I've read a couple of the articles on the sex things."

"Did you enjoy them?" Irene asked.

"What I could understand was okay," I answered.

I could see Henry Chaple giving Ms White some fairly speaking stares. Obviously I wasn't his favourite contestant.

"Why did you decide to enter the Ms Teeny-Wonderful contest?" was his next question.

Should I tell them how I wanted the honour of representing their wonderful magazine? No. I was doing well at cutting the bull. "I didn't decide to enter. My mother did. I had nothing to do with it," I admitted.

"So you came to Toronto because your mother wanted you to?" Irene said.

"Oh no, I came because I wanted to."

"Why?" Irene asked.

Should I continue telling the truth? Judging by Chaple's face I had nothing to lose anyway. "I want a trail bike."

"With the prize money?" Irene said.

"And a year off school."

"There will be a tutor," she insisted.

"Not the same thing," I pointed out.

"I guess not," she admitted.

"Hardly ideal reasons," Henry Chaple noted.

Irene started making notes on her clipboard. "What do you want to do when you finish school?" she asked as she wrote.

"Be a cop," I said without thinking about my answer.

"Thank you, Carol," Irene smiled briefly. "That will be all."

"What about the other questions?" Chaple asked her.

"I know enough already," announced the Editor-in-Chief.

"So do I," said Chaple, and I could certainly hear the negative feelings in that statement.

"May I go?" I asked.

"Certainly," Irene replied. "Enjoy your stay here and the coming events. I hope you take many happy memories of this competition back to St. Albert with you."

"Thank you," I said, smiling at both the editors.

"Oh," Irene said, looking at her clipboard, "I almost forgot. If you are chosen as one of the five grand finalists, what will your talent be?"

My expression must have matched my thoughts.

"Talent?" I said, feeling my anxiety rise.

"Yes," Irene answered. "What will you be performing?"

I looked at her, then at Henry Chaple. What was going on here? Surely they already knew what my talent was, or rather what What's-his-name's talent was—poetry. Were they trying to trick me? I remained dumb.

"Did we say something wrong?" Irene asked.

"No," I stuttered. "I was just curious about what you meant by talent." I decided to play along. "My mother said that my talent was poetry. That's what she said in the letter."

"That's right," said Irene. "Does that mean that you are going to recite your poem on a winter's morning?"

She knew what the poem was about. Were they about to reveal me as a fraud?

"The poem is very good," Irene was continuing. "In fact, it's exceptional. Is that what you want to do, recite it as your talent if you are chosen as a grand finalist?"

"No," I said.

"Fine." Irene wrote something else on her clipboard. "What do you wish to do then? Do you sing or play an instrument?"

She was letting me out of my copied poem. Without me trying, she had given me a way out of the embarrassment. All I had to do was tell her another talent and the copied poem would be history. My chest filled with an incredibly good feeling.

"I want to—" My mind drew a blank. What else could I do? It was true, what Wally had said two weeks before—I had no other talent.

"Yes," Henry Chaple said impatiently. "*What* do you want to do? Do you dance?"

I couldn't do anything except copy other people's poems.

"Well, what is it?" Irene demanded.

"I—er—" I really didn't have any other talents. "I jump garbage cans," I blurted out.

"Pardon me?" said Henry Chaple in surprise. "You jump garbage cans?"

"On my bike, on my BMX," I told them. "We lay garbage cans side by side, and then we build a ramp and we pedal like—like you know what—and then we jump over the cans."

"You jump over garbage cans on a bicycle?" It sounded as if Henry had never heard of it before.

"Not just any bike," I pointed out. "A bike has to be built to jump. It has to have wide handlebars, even ape-hangers, and strong front forks. Some kids go for a banana seat, but I prefer the BMX standard."

"Ape-hangers?" he uttered in disbelief. "Ms Weatherspoon, I'm sorry, but jumping over garbage cans on your bicycle is hardly what *Canada Woman* would consider a suitable talent for their Ms Teeny-Wonderful."

"Wait a moment, Henry," Irene said. "This is interesting. Carol, how popular is this garbage can jumping among kids?"

"Fairly," I said. "But it doesn't have to be just garbage cans. You can jump over everything or anything. Some kids jump over their friends."

"Do they?" Irene said. I could tell I was playing to a more attentive audience addressing her. "And how many girls do you think are into bike jumping?" she probed.

"Not as many as boys," I confessed. "But there are still quite a few. A lot of the really good jumpers are girls. They seem to have stronger nerves or something. You take Lois Granger—she goes to my school and she's a three-canner."

"A three-canner?" Irene asked.

"She's cleared three garbage cans without wiping out."

"Are you a three-canner?"

"I'm a five-canner. Wally and I are the only five-canners in St. Albert."

"Well, I must say that after all the interviews we've had this morning, yours is the most refreshing talent I've heard about."

"Irene, you can't be serious?" Henry Chaple snorted. "We can't have a Ms Teeny-Wonderful contestant who jumps over garbage cans! It just isn't a thing that girls do."

Irene shot the most effective dagger glare I had ever seen at her Promotion Editor. If she had been a teacher, every kid in the class would have been crawling under the seat. "I think it's a charming thing for a young girl to do," she said icily. "Carol, that sounds like a wonderful talent."

Chaple rolled his eyes.

"And Carol," Irene continued, "I think it's much better than that poem you wrote. I hope you won't mind my saying so, but your poem is very similar to others I've read. It is so hard to write something original, isn't it?"

"Yes," I agreed, "sometimes it really is difficult."

11
Sneaky switch

I had a good feeling after that interview with Mr. Chaple and Ms White. I knew that Henry was less than impressed with me, but at the same time I figured that Irene's feelings might outweigh his. Whatever, I had come out of the talk in better shape than I had gone in.

The incident at the banquet with the Campbell twins had been ironed over somewhat, and I had got out of that poem thing. It was obvious that Irene White had recognized the poem and had allowed me an honourable exit from my predicament. She was a fine lady.

As I changed my clothes I had to go through the interview three times for my mother before she seemed to catch on to what had happened. I left out the part about the copying of the poem and suggested that the editors had proposed that I try bike jumping because it was unique.

"They're going to let you jump your bike as your talent?" Mom said with the same puzzled tone as Henry Chaple.

"If I get chosen as one of the five grand finalists."

"They will actually let you jump over garbage cans?"

"Right, Mom," I insisted.

"Oh my!" she exclaimed. "Carol, this contest is certainly not going the way I thought it would."

Thank goodness for that, I thought to myself.

When I told Wally about my change of talent he took it much more calmly than my mother. To him, jumping garbage cans was a legitimate skill, something I did well. It was logical, therefore, that I should do it in the contest.

"I sure hope you get chosen as one of the grand finalists," was all he said. "I want to see you jump in the talent contest."

I ate a large lunch, feeling the best I had felt in days. Mom decided to go shopping in the afternoon. Wally decided to go up to the top of the CN Tower by himself. That left me with the entire afternoon to myself. I decided to spend it swimming in the hotel pool and sitting in the sauna. No need to get too ambitious.

I went down to the hotel recreational centre, entered the ladies' change room and slipped into my suit. There is one nice thing about staying in a large hotel—everything is so classy. The change room was actually carpeted. The walls were painted a deep pink, and one wall had floor-to-ceiling mirrors.

I had brought my tote bag downstairs with me. I tried to put it in one of the lockers, but unfortunately none of them had locks, which struck me as silly. Why provide the things if you're not going to provide locks? I didn't have anything really valuable, but I didn't want anybody coming in and rifling through my things and taking my watch and whatever. So I stuffed all my clothes into my bag and took it out with me.

I went to the sauna first. I stayed there until I couldn't breathe anymore, then took my bag, leaned it against the side of the wall and jumped into the pool for a nice long swim.

I must have wasted a good hour in the heated water, floating and swimming, watching other hotel guests come and go. Occasionally I'd dive to the bottom and enjoy the sensation of pressure on my eardrums. I wondered indifferently what Mom was going to buy and whether Wally had reached the top of that awful monstrosity yet.

Of course, all pleasant things must end, and my afternoon was spoiled by the appearance of the Campbell twins. I was alone in the pool when I saw them. They stood by the change room door, dressed in their matching bikini swimsuits. Even half-dressed they were just as gorgeous as they had been the night before. The bikinis must have been tailor-made as well, for they seemed to fit their skinny bodies perfectly. I say "skinny" out of jealousy. The twins' shapes matched their faces.

The one I assumed was Joan (she seemed a little shorter) looked down at me. "There's something dirty in the water," she announced.

"I see it," said Jean. "Look at the ring around the pool."

"It's no use swimming in here. Not with that in the water," Joan made a wrinkled face.

"It won't work, scumbutts," I smiled, crawling up the pool ladder. "You don't faze me at all. And furthermore, I suggest you don't bother me, because if you do I'll use your heads for bowling balls."

I picked up my bulging tote bag and walked toward the change room door. The twins backed off and went very silent. It made me happy to think that I could intimidate them into silence. As I pushed on the door I snarled at them and they gave a slight jump.

"Excuse me," Jean said quickly.

I shot her my best evil eye. She pointed at the door. "Wrong one," she said, smiling.

The sign on the door said *Men.* I let it close quickly, pulling a hasty retreat.

"Thanks," I said awkwardly as I pushed open the other door.

To this day I can't believe how dim-witted I was, thinking that the twins were trying to be nice. How could I have believed that either of them would do something nice for me? If I had had my old thinker on I would have realized that they had switched the signs on the doors. I still cringe when I think about how gullible I was.

As soon as the door closed behind me I heard some scraping on it. Even that didn't make me suspicious. Now I realize that they were changing the name plates back to their original positions.

I unpacked the crumpled contents of my bag and slipped my bathing suit off. I stood a moment looking at my wrinkled fingers and toes before I slipped on my underwear. I was kind of proud of myself for handling the twins when they had started to bug me. Little did I know.

I looked in the full-length mirror and started to brush my hair. Again I marvelled at the luxury of the change room—the pile carpet, the blue walls.

"Blue walls!" I said out loud.

At that second I caught on to what had happened. I slammed my fist against the lockers so hard that the noise hurt my ears. I'll kill them, I thought in my fury. Let me get dressed and I'll go out there and kill them!

I was reaching for my jeans when I heard the door open. Two loud and definitely male voices entered the change room. I darted into the toilet cubicle and slammed the door.

I sat on the seat in my underwear and listened to

the voices. They were talking about the Ms Teeny-Wonderful contest. It took only moments to recognize the whine of Henry Chaple.

"Oh no," I whispered to myself.

"Honestly, Ralph," Chaple was saying, "you people in advertising don't know how good you have it. This Teeny-Wonderful thing may have been a big mistake."

"I don't know about that, Henry," I heard Ralph reply. "We've had a lot of calls from national companies. Our ad revenue for the next month should be up twenty percent."

From the sounds I heard, I knew the men were changing into their swimsuits.

"I don't mean financially," Chaple went on. "Irene had that all figured out. It's bound to make money. I mean bringing fifty girls into one spot and expecting them to behave."

"Come on," Ralph said, "it isn't that bad. Except for the fight at the dinner last night, things have gone fairly well. I think the girls are acting fine."

Chaple let loose a big sigh. "You're right, Ralph. It has only been that one barbarian, Carol What's-her-spoon. But there's a lot of craziness in that one. And it's like that old saying: 'One bad apple spoils the whole bunch.'"

"I think you're over-reacting," Ralph pointed out.

"Over-reacting!" Chaple snapped. "Do you know

what that little monster wants to do for her talent?"

"Punch somebody out?" Ralph chuckled.

"Now that wouldn't surprise me," Chaple said. "The truth is—you are not going to believe this, Ralph—the little she-devil wants to jump her bicycle over garbage cans. I'd like to stick her in a garbage can and ship her back to St. Arthur."

St. Albert, I almost called out.

"The thing is," Chaple continued his harangue, "Irene thinks that it could be a good idea to let her do it. You know, liberated girls doing liberated things."

"I don't know," Ralph said. "It doesn't sound so bad to me. Most contests like this are boring. Lots of giggling people performing mediocre talent. I think a bike jump would liven things up."

Good insight, Ralph, I thought.

"That's why *you're* not Promotion Editor," Chaple told him.

I could hear him walking toward the door of the cubicle. After listening to his comments, I was tempted to open the door and give him a piece of my mind. But how could I give anybody heck dressed in my underwear?

"Are you finished in there?" I heard Henry saying. But all I could think of was how I wished he and Ralph would hurry and leave so that I could get out of that change room.

"I said, are you almost finished in there?" There

was irritation in Chaple's voice. I realized that he was calling to me.

I lowered my voice as low as it would go and let out a long, "No."

"Are you going to be much longer?" he asked.

Again in my deepest tone, I answered, "Yeah, gonna be long."

"Come on, Henry," Ralph said. "Let's go for that swim. You said you have more interviews at four o'clock."

"I can't," the Promotion Editor explained. "I have to go to the washroom first. It's a thing with me. Every time I get in the water I have to take a—"

"Gonna be a long time," I growled again, not wanting to hear about Henry Chaple's swimming difficulties.

"Hey, Henry, look at this," Ralph declared. "There's a tote bag and a girl's blouse on the floor. Funny, huh?"

"Yes," Chaple said impatiently, "real funny. Which is more than I can say for this person in here. Come on, hurry up!"

I heard the door to the change room open once more. Oh no, I thought. Here's how to make a bad situation worse.

"Hello," drawled a new voice.

I felt my heart begin to pound. I recognized that greeting.

"Excuse me, have you been here long?" Wally asked Chaple and Ralph.

"Seems that way," moaned the Promotion Editor.

"Hey!" Wally said with profound amazement. "I know who you are. You're that editor guy for *Canada Woman* magazine, the one with the tight jeans."

"I beg your pardon?" Chaple huffed.

"The tight jeans," Wally repeated. "I was talking to the Pit about you this morning. Gosh, your pants are tight. How do you fit into them? Doesn't it hurt when you bend over?"

"Young man," Chaple said coolly, "my clothes are hardly a topic that I wish to discuss with a boy who obviously needs a haircut."

Wally kept rolling. "My older sister Paula, she's fifteen. She always puts on her jeans when they're still a little wet. That way they dry real tight."

"Fascinating," Chaple said sarcastically. "I fail to see how I lived without that totally absorbing fact."

"Thanks," Wally said. "That's real nice of you. I'll tell my sister. She'll think it was a nice thing for you to say."

Chaple exhaled deeply and knocked impatiently on the cubicle door. "Please hurry up," he said.

"Are you going swimming?" Wally asked.

"No," answered Chaple. "We're changing into our swimsuits so we can eat lunch."

"Yeah?" mumbled Wally. "You magazine people sure do lead an exciting life."

"What exactly do you want?" snarled Chaple.

"Oh," drawled Wally, "I'm looking for somebody. I dropped in to ask if you'd seen her. She said she'd be swimming in the pool. You'd know her—she was the one who flew across the table at dinner last night."

"We haven't been in the pool yet," announced Ralph. "Come on, Henry."

"I've seen her," I growled. "Your five-canner buddy is close by." I hoped that Wally would recognize the clue.

"Who's in there?" he asked stupidly.

"So you're looking for the barbarian?" Chaple said.

"Do you know Carol?" Wally probed, ignoring the Promotion Editor.

"Very well," I said in my deepest voice. "Very well indeed. You could say we are really close. I know that she's afraid of flying and elevators, and that she's going to kill two pretty little twins when she gets a chance."

"If you want to talk about the little witch, then get out of the toilet and let me in," Henry pleaded.

"Are you who I think you are?" Wally asked.

How long does it take for something to get through that thick hair? "Yeah," I said, "it's me. And I want to get out."

"Well, come on out!" Henry's voice was raised in exasperation.

"What do you need?" Wally asked.

"I need my jeans and my bl— I mean shirt," I explained.

"Hang on," he said, and I could hear him going across the room and gathering up my clothes. A few seconds later they came flying over the door. I dressed quickly.

"You meet the strangest people in the strangest places," Wally said.

"I've noticed," Chaple mused.

I took a deep breath and flung the door open.

"What in—" Chaple gasped.

The Promotion Editor and his friend Ralph were standing in their swimsuits, their mouths open. Wally smiled and nodded as if it was normal for me to be in the toilet cubicle of the men's change room.

"Excuse me," I said to Henry Chaple. "I'm sorry to have kept you waiting. It was very barbarian of me."

Neither of the two men spoke. They watched me gather my tote bag with puzzled, dumbfounded stares.

"Once again I apologize for the inconvenience," I said in my sweetest Ms Teeny-Wonderful voice.

As I exited from the room, I could hear Chaple muttering, "I knew it was a mistake."

I turned to Wally with hatred in my heart.

“Where can I get a bazooka, Wally?” I snarled.

Of course the twins were not around anymore, which was fortunate for them. I was seething. I was probably more angry at myself for being fooled by such an obvious prank, but whatever, I was livid. It was a good thing that Wally was around to talk with me until I cooled off.

“I don’t believe it,” I yelled. “How could they do that to me? How could I be so stupid?”

“We all do stupid things,” Wally announced.

“I’m going to get even, you know,” I vowed. “For sure I’m going to get them for this.”

“The CN Tower was neat,” Wally said trying to change the subject.

“Who cares!” I screamed.

“All right,” he said. “I’m your friend, remember?”

I knew that I had hurt him. Sometimes I get so caught up in my own troubles that I forget about how I’m affecting other people. Wally was only trying to calm me down.

“Sorry, Wal,” I said as we walked through the lobby to the elevators. “Tell me about the concrete marvel.”

“It’s so high you can see for an awful long way,” he began quickly. “You can see all down Lake Ontario and you can see the city of Hamilton.”

Big thrill, I thought.

“And you can see the spray from Niagara Falls.

That's over a hundred kilometres away."

Bigger thrill. All of this didn't sound too exciting, and it didn't take my mind off the twins at all.

"The elevator ride was something else," Wally continued. "With all your talk about elevator cables and stuff, I was a little scared myself. Even falling only part of the way down would sure turn one of those elevators into a mess of steel and people."

The doors of the hotel elevator opened. I gave Wally a long, thoughtful look. "*That* took my mind off the Campbells," I announced. "It also made me decide to walk to my room."

"It's twelve stories," Wally pointed out.

"A long way to fall," I said.

12
Mummies' revenge

Our big Teeny-Wonderful dance was that evening in the Simcoe Room. In spite of my desire to fake being sick so that I wouldn't have to go, the event turned out all right.

There were lots of TV cameras around, a live rock band and a stand-up snack bar. Wally didn't want to dance, which suited me just fine. Mom managed to coax us onto the floor a few times though, just so we would have our chance in front of the cameras. I saw the twins and their escorts, but they managed to stay on the other side of the ballroom.

During a slow dance, while Wally and I were holding each other awkwardly and taking turns stepping on each other's feet, we talked about the museum visit that was scheduled for the next morning.

"I'm not sure I can go to the museum and enjoy myself, knowing the Parade of Charm and the choosing of the finalists are going to happen in the afternoon," I confessed.

"I guess it is kind of scary," Wally agreed.

"Museums don't exactly turn me on," I continued.

"Maybe it'll be different tomorrow. The museum has a special display on. It's a loan of artifacts from some famous museum in Egypt. There are all kinds of Egyptian treasures on display, plus a lot of mummies."

"Mummies?" I said. "They moved mummies?"

"Yeah," Wally informed me. "Don't you ever watch the news?"

"Of course I don't watch the news," I snapped. "It's all about plane crashes."

"The exhibit is world famous," Wally explained. "People are lining up for hours just to get tickets to get in. That's why visiting the museum is such a big thing for this contest. It's real newsworthy."

I wondered why people would bother to ship dried-out bodies across the world. And I wondered even more why they would line up to see them. "Mummies give me the creeps," I announced.

"A lot of people say that," Wally noted. "Apparently these mummies were chosen because they show different aspects of the mummification technique, especially the different ways of wrapping the bandages."

"Where do you get all this stuff from?" I asked.

Then the first words he had said sank into my brain. A lot of people *were* queasy or even frightened of mummies. I had a sudden idea.

"Hey, Wal," I said quickly. "Will you help me get back at the twins?"

He pulled away from me. "Will it be legal?"

"Yeah," I nodded. "It'll just involve a bit of acting and a bit of dressing up."

"I don't like the sound of that."

"Oh, it'll be a breeze. All you'll have to do is stand and groan a lot. You're pretty good at doing that anyway."

"What's that mean?"

"Nothing. Come on, Wally. I think it'll be perfect. We'll need some bandages though. What time is that drugstore in the hotel lobby open until?"

"Eleven, I think. But what do we need bandages for? What do you have in mind?"

"Trust me," I said. "Trust me."

After the dance had finished I went with Wally to his room and explained the full plan to him. At first he thought my idea was ridiculous and stupid, but finally I had him convinced that if we could pull it off it would be a wonderful stunt.

The Pit was eating a large, loaded pizza during our conversation. Between slices he announced that he would be willing to help Wally get dressed and do whatever else he could.

"Thanks a lot, Pit," I said. "You guys could do one

other thing before you go to sleep."

"What?" Wally asked suspiciously.

"You could go downstairs and mess up those bandages we bought," I replied. "A three-thousand-year-old body wouldn't be wrapped in nice white bandages, would it?"

* * *

The next morning a bus picked up the Ms Teeny-Wonderful contestants and their escorts from the Hotel Ontario for the museum visit. Because of the limited space inside the special Egyptian exhibit, moms were not invited. Only five chaperone-hostesses from *Canada Woman* magazine accompanied us.

Mom wasn't too upset about missing the museum visit. She declared that the time would be well spent if she stayed in the hotel room and got everything ready for the afternoon's competition. Of course I was pleased; not having mothers along would help to ensure the smooth running of my plan.

Wally looked a little obvious carrying his shopping bag onto the bus, but probably only to me. Besides the Pit, I was the only one who knew what he was taking along for our special tour.

It took about ten minutes in city traffic to arrive at the museum. Television cameras met us as we disembarked from the bus and made our way through the entrance and into the special exhibit. As a museum guide gave us an introductory speech about the exhibit we were about to see, the cameras recorded our expressions. With the contest finals coming up, we did our best to appear suitably impressed.

I moved through the exhibit listening to the knowledgeable ramblings of the guide with one ear. The rest of my attention was given to seeing how I could make my plan work.

The exhibit was divided into sections by partitions and display cases. That was as I had expected. In fact, it was perfect. As we passed the washrooms, I directed Wally into the men's room. The Pit followed him. He had informed Lucy that he would be missing for a little while.

The next step was to get the twins isolated from the rest of the group. No easy task, but I had thought of a couple of plans the night before. As we were clustered around some Canopic jars, I managed to sidle up to either Jean or Joan's escort. I reached over and shook his hand.

"Hi," I whispered. "I'm Carol."

He returned the handshake with reluctance, not knowing what to make of my offer of friendship. He mumbled a greeting and told me his name was Dale.

"Well, Dale," I continued, "I wonder if you'd do me a favour?"

He squinted his eyes with suspicion.

"Seriously," I said, sugar-coating my words. "You know that Jean and Joan and I have had a few—let's say misunderstandings —between us."

He nodded, a silly grin spreading across his face.

"Well," I said, "I want to make up with them. I don't want it to go on any longer and jeopardize our chances of winning."

He raised his eyebrows.

"I don't want to be their friend or anything," I assured him. That much was true. "I just want a truce."

"So what do you want me to do about it?" Dale snarled.

It was taking all of my patience to talk nicely to this turkey, but it had to be done to make the plan work.

"I'd like you to tell Jean and Joan to meet me back there by the pottery display so I can talk to them."

"Don't think they'll do it," Dale announced. "They're afraid you'll beat them up."

I held up my hand. "Word of honour—I won't touch them." That much was true as well. "If they don't trust me, you can bring your buddy and come along to protect them."

Dale snorted. "I'll tell them," he said. "But don't bet on them coming."

As the guide moved to the next display case, I

watched Dale turn to the twins. They had noticed me talking to him, but in the large group, with the tour guide speaking over our whispers, they couldn't have heard what I was saying.

I was counting on two things. First, that the twins would think I was too stupid to retaliate in any other way than with violence, and second, that curiosity to find out what I'd say would make them break away from the group.

I wended my way back through the exhibit and knocked on the men's washroom door. The Pit opened it and looked at me. "Ready?" he asked.

I nodded and watched the door close momentarily. When it opened again, the Pit guided Wally out.

Wally was perfect. I had thought that when he was wrapped in bandages the result would be more humorous than frightening. More like one of those bandaged accident victims in comedy shows than an authentic mummy. But Wally was a reasonable facsimile. Whatever they had done to the bandages had made them look realistically ancient, and they clung so tightly to his body that he appeared to have been wrapped for thousands of years.

"Pine tar," the Pit answered my unasked question. "We smeared the wrappings in pine tar. Makes him look old and helps them stick to his body."

"It smells a bit too," I noted.

"Can't have everything," the Pit smiled.

Wally moved forward awkwardly. It was clear that he couldn't bend his arms and legs in all that wrapping. Thinking of my friend dressed up inside all those bandages made me smile.

"Boy, if the kids could see you now," I said.

He mumbled something through the face wrappings.

"You look like you just tried to jump seven cans and didn't make it." I started to chuckle.

"I don't want to seem pushy," interrupted the Pit, "but if you want to fool those twins, don't you think we should get into position?"

"Right," I said. Joan and Jean, if they were coming, would appear at any moment. "Stand behind that partition with the pottery fragments on it," I instructed. "I'll stand to the left so that the twins will be looking at the mummy display behind me. Give me a little time, then do your thing."

Wally nodded, mumbled and hobbled with the Pit toward the partition. I went and assumed my position. I could hear the crowd further on in the exhibit. I watched for my two adversaries.

A minute passed and the Campbell sisters didn't show. Another minute. I was beginning to get anxious. Perhaps their curiosity wasn't as great as I thought.

And then I heard their footsteps coming slowly. They inched around a display case, looking cautiously at me.

"If you try to hit us, we'll scream so loud that everybody will come running, and we'll say that you attacked us without warning," Joan threatened.

I held open my arms. "Hey," I said, "this is an attempt to make up for the hassles. I realize that you were just teasing me and that it was all in good fun."

"It wasn't," said Jean. "We don't like you."

"Well, the feeling is mutual," I confessed. "But let's not let it ruin our chances of winning, huh? Let's call it quits."

"Let's go," snarled Joan. "She doesn't have anything to say to us."

"Then you're not interested in sorting things out?" I asked.

"Not with you," said Jean. "Let me give you a brief description of the real world. Some people are always winners. They were born that way. Some people are losers. They, too, were born that way. Joan and I are winners. We can't help it, it's just the way things turned out. You are a loser. That, too, is a fact that nobody can do anything about. You're wasting our time."

Boy, would I have liked to take a baseball bat to their ears. Instead I put my plan into action. "What's that noise?" I said, letting as much mock concern filter into my voice as I could.

They looked at me, wondering what I was doing.

"You didn't hear something?" I turned around and looked at the mummies in their cases behind me.

"This place gives me the creeps," I said, and walked quickly past them, heading toward the Teeny-Wonderful tour.

As I had hoped, the twins watched me go, yelling "Sucky baby" at the same time.

Wally timed his entrance perfectly. Stiffly, he rounded the pottery partition, giving a superb imitation of a demonic growl. The twins whirled around. I turned too, to watch the scene. Oh, what I would have given to be able to see their faces at that instant! How does one react when confronted by a walking body that has been dead for three thousand years?

They ripped around and went scrambling through the exhibit. Their mouths were open and their eyes literally bulged from their heads. I smiled as they ran past me, too frightened to even utter a warning, their peachy complexions deathly white. My plan so far was working perfectly.

The Pit was already rolling the bandages off Wally when I trotted back to them. "Give us two minutes and we'll be back," he said as he directed my friend to the washroom.

I hurried back toward the group of Ms Teeny-Wonderful contestants where they were standing just at the exit of the special exhibit.

By the buzz of confusion I could tell that the Campbell sisters had arrived. They were both talking rapidly, trying to describe what they had seen to the guide and the *Canada Woman* chaperones. All that seemed to be coming out of their mouths was "mummy, large, run, awful" and other similar, disjointed words.

The TV cameras had been set up at the exit to film the contestants coming out of the exhibit. They were catching the whole scene. The blubbering, whimpering twins were being recorded on film. I felt wonderful.

One of the chaperones, a large woman, tried to take control of the situation. "Stop it this instant," she said to the twins. "We will not put up with this silliness. Mummies do not walk about."

Wally appeared, minus his wrappings but still smelling like cleaning detergent. He and the Pit moved in beside me. "All clear," Wally whispered. They should have a section in the *Guinness Book of World Records* for the shortest time unwrapping a mummy.

"It's working perfectly," I whispered.

Now it was time to put the finishing touch on my little trick. I moved to the girl nearest me and whispered into her ear. "I don't think their little trick is working very well," I said. "They probably thought it would be funny to try to scare the rest of us. I think their plan failed."

It was all that was necessary. The girl I had spoken to passed it on to her neighbour and soon it was all through the crowd. As I had assumed, my statement became more true as it travelled around. Soon it was being passed as fact that the Campbell twins were playing a trick on us. By the time the rumour got back to me, it was told with a certain amount of anger.

The guide went back and did a quick tour of the gallery. She returned to us, shrugged her shoulders and said, "Nothing," to the large chaperone.

"As I thought," the lady snapped. "Joan and Jean Campbell, your little plan to scare us has not worked. It has, in fact, only embarrassed you in front of your fellow contestants and the cameras. This is not appropriate behaviour for a Ms Teeny-Wonderful contestant."

I loved it. What a nasty person I was. I watched their puzzled, frightened and embarrassed expressions and I loved it.

Shame on me.

13
Dale's dirty deed

When the Teeny-Wonderful contestants returned to the Hotel Ontario, Mom was waiting to deck me out in the prettiest of the dresses we had purchased before the contest. She listened with interest as I recounted the twins' embarrassment at the museum, omitting my part in the happenings, of course. "I guess their little tricks finally got them into trouble," she mused.

Wally and the Pit decided to go downstairs to the restaurant for lunch, but Mom and I ordered a couple of salmon sandwiches from room service.

"You should see what they've done to the room downstairs," exclaimed Mother. "They've opened up a dividing wall to make it even bigger now, and they've put up a stage at one end with curtains all around it and lots of flowers. Oh, it's so pretty. The TV cameras are set up, and I saw Terry Howard, the master of ceremonies, rehearsing a few of the musical numbers with the dancers. It's going to be wonderful."

"Teeny-Wonderful," I said.

"Carol, this is what I dreamed of when I sent that application away to *Canada Woman* magazine. I hoped that you would be chosen so that you and I could be here to experience this."

"The bread is stale," I announced, biting into my sandwich.

"Carol," she smiled, "I realize that you are extremely nervous and that you are trying to cope by pretending not to care about the contest. That's all right, I understand."

I'm glad she did. I thought I was taking things quite coolly. My dealings with the twins that morning had taken the nervous edge from the competition. I was looking forward to the afternoon's events.

Mom picked up her tea and began walking toward the washroom. "I'm going to get ready. The Parade of Charm is at two o'clock," she reminded me as she went.

I was taking another bite of the stale sandwich when I heard her cry out in anguish. "*Aaaaagh*!"

I jumped to my feet, nearly choking on the food. It took only a second to notice what had made my mother scream. She stood by the bed where my dress was laid out, half a cup of tea in her hand. The other half had made a splash pattern all over the dress.

My mother was almost as white as the Campbell sisters had been earlier. "It was an accident," she whispered. "I tripped. It was an accident."

"It's okay, Mom," I assured her.

Actually it wasn't. I was getting into this contest thing now. My initial reaction had softened considerably. Now I could even picture myself being the first-ever Ms Teeny-Wonderful and enjoying it. Enjoying more than just the dirt bike and the year off.

We had spent a great deal of time looking for the perfect dress for me to wear in the Parade of Charm. We had discovered this one at the last store we searched. Not only did it fit me perfectly, but the warm brown colour seemed to bring out highlights in my hair. It was as if I had found a fashion designer to make it just for me. I had been counting on it to help me win a place as a grand finalist.

"It's okay, Mom," I repeated unenthusiastically. "I'll wear the same one I did at the dance last night."

My mother started to cry.

"Maybe we could get it cleaned," I suggested without much hope.

Mom wiped her eyes. "The hotel laundry," she smiled. "There's a sign in the lobby that says one-hour dry cleaning." She looked at her watch. "Oh, Carol, you're wonderful."

Ms Teeny-Wonderful, I thought.

* * *

I left the hotel room with my soiled dress and hurried toward the elevator, suppressing the fear that wouldn't leave me after Wally's words about the CN Tower. One of the room doors near the elevator swung open as I passed, and out marched Dale with a pair of grey slacks over his arm.

I froze, not knowing what to do. I was ready to drop the dress and start defending myself against an outraged foe, but instead of a snarl, his face broke into a broad grin. Not the silly one he had given me at the dinner and the museum. This was a genuine amused grin.

"Carol," he said, "I was hoping I could speak to you before the contest."

"Why?" It was my turn to be suspicious.

"Because," he chuckled. "Because of that great trick you played on Jean and Joan. It was priceless. I couldn't stop laughing. You made them look like a couple of jackasses."

This didn't make sense.

"Hey," Dale continued, "they had it coming. They've been really nasty to you, and to some of the other girls too. They deserved it."

"That doesn't sound like a nice way to speak about your girlfriend," I probed.

"Girlfriend!" he said, almost choking on the

word. "Get real! Do I look like I'd want Joan Campbell to be my girlfriend? Bart and I are the twins' second cousins. We're here only because our moms made us come."

I was still dubious.

"Look," he pleaded, "all hard feelings behind us. I won't fool with you any more, I promise. Friends, okay?"

What was I supposed to say? "Okay," I murmured without enthusiasm.

Dale looked at my dress. "You going to the laundry?"

I nodded.

"Me too. Gotta get these pants pressed before the big parade. I'll walk with you, okay?"

"Okay," I agreed. What did I have to lose?

"Better yet," Dale suggested, "I'll take your stuff down and bring it up to you when it's finished. That way you can start putting your make-up on and all that."

"I don't know," I said, suspicious once more.

"Come on," he scoffed. "What am I going to do, steal the dress? Have a little faith."

I could use the extra time, I thought. I had to wash my hair and let Mom get it curled properly. But still...

At that moment the elevator door opened. A chance to miss two elevator rides was nothing to sneeze at. "Okay," I agreed. "I'm in room twelve eighteen."

"Sure," Dale smiled. "Trust me," he said as he stepped into the elevator. "It'll all work out."

I went back to our room and told Mom of my meeting with Dale and his offer of a favour. She just passed off my comments and pushed me into the shower with the shampoo. "Good, let's use the time. If you're going to look pretty for the parade, we have a lot of work to do," she proclaimed.

"Thanks for the compliment," I replied.

But while I was getting myself ready I grew more and more suspicious of Dale. Without that open elevator door staring at me, it was harder to believe he'd been sincere. If I hadn't been tricked by the twins at the swimming pool I probably wouldn't have given the favour a second thought. But now I was wary of good deeds that originated from or around the Campbell sisters.

I was surprised, therefore, when a hotel bellboy brought my dress, neatly packaged in dry-cleaning plastic, to our door. "A young man asked me to bring this up," the bellboy announced. "He said he was busy and would see you at the Teeny-thing later."

My faith in the human race was restored. I felt miserable that I had doubted Dale's good intentions.

"Mom, my dress is here," I called.

"Oh good," Mom exclaimed, picking up the dress

and ripping off the plastic covering. “Let’s see how well they got rid of that tea stain.”

As the last of the plastic dropped to the floor we stared at the dress with stunned expressions.

“Damn!” I said.

“Carol,” Mother scolded, “I will not tolerate that language!”

“Look at the dress, Mom!” I yelled. “Look what they’ve done to my dress!”

The tea stain had been removed perfectly; there was no sign of the accident. The cleaning had been worthless, however, for the material was slashed into ribbons. It appeared as if someone had taken a knife to the dress and simply started ripping until his or her hand became tired. Which is probably what had happened.

“Oh dear,” said Mother.

14
Giggles and glamour

The events in the Simcoe Room of the Hotel Ontario that afternoon would make up the bulk of the *Teeny-Wonderful Special* to be shown on TV later that evening. Pre-recorded segments from the supper, dance and museum trip would be added in as fillers while the judges made their decisions.

The actual contest itself would be short for most girls. The master of ceremonies, Terry Howard, would introduce each of the fifty contestants. As he did, we would walk down a carpeted ramp with our escorts, stop in front of a camera for a few seconds while the audience got a good look at us, then move backstage again.

The judges were to score us on the basis of our poise and choice of fancy dress. These marks, together with the grades we had received from Irene White and Henry Chaple, would determine the five grand finalists. The contestants, without their escorts, would stand on risers on the stage to hear the judges' decision. About an hour later the top five would perform their talents. The one who got the highest score on that would be Ms Teeny-Wonderful.

Wally and I stood forty-eighth in the line of contestants behind the stage. I glared twenty couples ahead at the blonde heads of Joan and Jean Campbell. I was dressed in the same outfit I had worn to the dance the previous night. It wasn't bad, but it certainly didn't match the frills and fussiness of the other contestants' dresses. I felt like the poor relation of the Teeny-Wonderful family. No doubt I would have felt much worse if it weren't for my seething anger at the Campbell jerks.

"You look real nice," Wally tried to flatter me.

"Nice yes," I grumbled, "but not great. Look at the other girls. Some of them look gorgeous."

"That's true," Wally agreed. "But remember that the dress-up thing is judged on poise, not on gorgeousness."

"Poise," I sneered. "What does poise mean? It's just a fancy way of saying good looks. It makes feminists less upset if *Canada Woman* says they're judging on poise instead of beauty, but really it's the same thing."

"Could be," drawled Wally.

I reached up and pushed his bangs away from his eyes. They immediately fell back into place. "How could anybody be so cruel? How could they be so downright nasty?" I growled. "They deliberately ripped up my dress so that I'd have less of a chance. That isn't a prank. It isn't even a nasty trick. It's cruel behaviour. It's cheating."

"I agree," Wally nodded. "But it's natural, you know."

One of the chaperone-hostesses moved down the line. "The emcee is introducing the show," she said. "Get ready. We'll start parading in front of the cameras in a minute."

"What's natural?" I asked, staring at Wally.

"Cruelty, cheating. It's natural," he responded.

Wally always had a way of sidetracking my anger by talking about strange and unusual things. This time I was determined not to lose my fury. I would refuse to carry Wally's statements any further. I would let them lie.

My determination lasted five seconds. "Okay, tell me why cruelty is natural," I said through clenched teeth.

"Just look at nature," Wally rambled. "It's cruel. Aren't animals always eating other animals? That's cruel. I heard about a spider that pretends it's an ant. When a real ant comes close, it eats him. And then there's the black widow spider. Did you know she eats her mate? That's kind of cruel."

"Kind of," I said.

"I also heard there's a kind of monkey that, if the

head male of a troop dies, the male who takes his place will kill all the other male's babies. That's sort of cruel."

"Sort of," I said.

"I also heard of a type of wasp that paralyzes a whole bunch of spiders and insects, then lays its eggs on them and seals them all in a nest. When the egg hatches, the larva eats the insects while they're still alive. That's kind of cruel too."

"Kind of," I said. "Get to the point."

Wally shrugged. "Oh, I'm just saying that cruelty is natural for animals and you shouldn't be surprised to see it in people."

"Of course I'm surprised," I nearly shouted. "We're supposed to be civilized people living in a civilized country. We play fair. That's what makes everything work. We play fair, we don't try to mess up another person just out of spite."

Wally nodded, but even though I couldn't see his eyes I knew that he didn't agree with me. I was about to continue my line of reasoning when the chaperone came hurrying down the line.

"We're on, people," she said. "Get ready. Here we go."

We were hustled forward so that the tip of the line was standing near the back curtain of the stage. Another chaperone was standing near the slit in the curtain with her hand outstretched. From where we stood we could hear the speech of the golden-throated emcee.

Terry Howard used to be a famous radio DJ back in the fifties. He graduated to TV as a game show host in the States, and since that time has become known as "Canada's emcee." Every time there's, an award show to host or a beauty contest to emcee, there's good old Terry Howard smiling through his teeth.

"And now, ladies and gentlemen, boys and girls," we heard him announce, "we proudly present our Ms Teeny-Wonderful finalists and their escorts in the Parade of Charm.

"Remember, folks, each of these girls has chosen her dress personally. Our judges will be marking them on their choice, as well as on their charm and poise. These marks will be combined with the marks given by the editors of *Canada Woman* magazine when they interviewed the girls yesterday. The result will tell us who our five grand finalists are.

"Are you ready?" Old Terry's throat was at its best. It was impossible not to be excited. "Let's start with Ms Lucy Dragrett from Yellowknife, Northwest Territories."

The chaperone parted the curtain. I could see the Pit's head move forward, but I didn't catch a glimpse of Lucy.

There was a fifteen second pause before Howard crooned, "Ms Joyce Mullins from Brandon, Manitoba." Again the curtain parted.

Wally and I shuffled forward slowly. My hands were beginning to sweat as I heard each girl announced and saw her vanish through the curtain. Eventually the twins stood at the front of the line.

"And now, contestant number twenty-seven is a special treat," Howard laid on the sugar. "Number twenty-seven is not one, but two lovely girls. From our capital city, Joan and Jean Campbell."

I wanted to upchuck. I could just imagine them trotting down the ramp, smiling and looking so innocent, just as they always did when the eyes of the world were on them. The audience seemed to clap more loudly for them than they had for the other contestants. How disgusting.

We shuffled forward another pace.

I looked up at Wally and found him staring back at me—as much as he could. "Nervous?" he asked.

I nodded.

"Got a joke then," he said.

Save me, I thought.

"Mommy, Mommy, what's a werewolf?"

I gave him my best bored look.

"Shut up and comb your face," he said in his best imitation of a mother's voice.

Now I looked at him in disbelief. "You're kidding."

"I've got more," he announced. "Mommy, Mommy, what's a vampire?"

"You've *got* to be kidding."

In his best mother voice again, "Shut up and drink your blood."

"I don't believe it," I said.

"Got more," he chuckled. "Mommy, Mommy, I don't like spaghetti."

Again the mother, "Shut up or I'll rip the—"

"You're next," an impatient voice interrupted. We looked at the chaperone. "Terry Howard is calling your name," she said. "Get out there!"

I heard old Golden Throat finishing the intro, "... eatherspoon from St. Albert, Alberta."

Wally and I trotted through the curtain and started down the ramp. I had been afraid that I would be unable to look at the audience and watch their faces when they saw my relatively plain dress. But the footlights and TV lights were so bright that I couldn't even see the cameras, let alone the people sitting beyond them.

I held on to Wally's elbow, giving my best smile. Then Wally's joke hit me. I knew I had heard it before. Who hasn't heard those Mommy, Mommy jokes? But until that time I had never really thought about it. Now I could picture this little werewolf kid asking his big werewolf mommy what the heck a werewolf was.

I started to laugh. Not just giggle. I mean I started to laugh a big gut-wobbling guffaw. It must have been my nervousness.

And then I thought of the little vampire kid and his bowl of blood. My eyes started to water and I staggered. Wally looked at me, shook his blond hair and started to giggle.

When we stopped on the landing in front of the TV camera for our close-up, we were both laughing so hard that neither one of us could stand up properly. We bounced off one another's shoulders and almost fell. I could hear a few nervous giggles from the audience (probably my mother's), and then polite handclapping as we moved away and Howard introduced the next contestant.

Another chaperone met us as we moved offstage, but we were beyond listening to anything she might have said.

"What's so funny?" Wally laughed, unable to control himself. "What's so funny?"

I couldn't stop laughing long enough to tell him.

We had been told that after all the contestants had had their turn on stage, Terry Howard would introduce the judges and then a dance routine by a Toronto young people's jazz company. After that we would take our places on the risers for the announcement of the five grand finalists.

In the meantime, we were to wait behind the stage. Most of the girls crowded quietly around the monitors that had been placed backstage. I stood against the wall, still having little fits of giggling.

"We blew it," I said. "For sure, we just blew it."

"Naw," Wally drawled, "we just looked happy, that's all. It may work in your favour."

"Happy," I laughed. "I nearly wet my pants on national TV. We looked more than happy."

"I guess," Wally agreed.

I could see one of the twins watching us from the safety of a group of contestants. I couldn't tell which one it was. She had a silly half-grin on her face, as if she knew what I was telling Wally—that we were out of the running.

I gave her a little wave. I was still angry, but there was very little chance of punching their noses right then, so why not be silly?

What little chatter there was within the group stopped suddenly as the Editor-in-Chief of *Canada Woman* entered our midst. She looked severely around the room, making a few formal smiles. It was obvious that she was looking for someone. I felt a little lump grow in my throat when she spotted me and began walking briskly over.

Irene stopped in front of us and stared into my eyes without speaking. I felt like Anne Boleyn waiting for the executioner's axe to fall on my neck.

"Carol," she said, "I just wanted to tell you that I thought your choice of dress this afternoon was excellent."

I exhaled deeply.

"Considering that the other girls chose to dress in fancy attire, I felt that your more simple approach made a definite impression. I think you will score highly with our judges. I chose them, you know, and I think I understand what they like."

"Thank you," I said meekly.

"Now," she said sternly, "what was so funny?"

"I'm sorry I laughed," I said. "But Wally had been telling me these jokes, and they suddenly hit me and...I know it was silly of me."

"Nonsense," she smiled. "I'm glad to see you having fun."

As Irene walked away I noticed that most of the eyes of the other contestants and escorts were focused on me. From the smirks on the faces of the Campbells, I could tell that they thought I had just got grand heck from the boss.

I looked at them blankly, giving nothing away. Inside I felt that Irene White was pulling for me, that I had a chance.

15
The final five

The forty-nine other contestants and I stood on the risers, smiling at the camera that panned across our faces. We were waiting for the decision of the judges so we would know whether to start packing our bags or rehearsing our talents.

We stood minus our escorts, and I realized how much I had come to rely on Wally's presence during the last couple of days. The contest was for Ms Teeny-Wonderful, but I had been thinking that Wally and I were in it together. Standing out in front of the TV lights without my friend made me feel uncomfortable. I wasn't sure that I could face the decision without Wally.

"And now, ladies and gentlemen, boys and girls," old Golden Throat, Terry Howard, announced, "here is the list of our five grand finalists." He held up a piece of paper for the audience and contestants to see.

"The five names on this list represent the girls who obtained the highest points from our judges during the Parade of Charm and most impressed the editors of *Canada Woman* magazine during the personal interviews. I won't keep you in suspense any longer. Here are the five grand finalists for the title of Ms Teeny-Wonderful."

I sucked in my breath and squinted into the lights, hoping to see my mother. It was too bright. I could make out the shape of the whole audience, but all individuality was lost.

"Our first finalist," sang out Howard, "... Lucy Dragrett from Yellowknife, Northwest Territories."

I broke into spontaneous applause. I had never met Lucy; I don't think I could have picked her out from the other contestants. But I knew the Pit and I was happy for him. I watched a blonde-haired girl in the front row skip toward the emcee.

"Our second grand finalist, from Brantford, Ontario...Cher Obediah."

I clapped for the dark-haired girl who stepped carefully down the risers toward Howard. She gave Lucy a big hug.

That was two, which meant there were only three names left to be called.

"From Sydney, Nova Scotia, our third grand finalist...Susan Hopkins."

Susan stepped eagerly from the risers.

"Our fourth grand finalist is really two people," Howard crooned.

Oh no, I thought. How could the judges be so stupid?

"From Ottawa, Ontario...Joan and Jean Campbell."

The applause made me want to walk down and say, "Come off it, people." I felt spit build in my mouth as Joan and Jean gave cute little hugs to Golden Throat.

"And our last grand finalist"—Howard paused—"from St. Albert, Alberta...Carol Weatherspoon."

I stood frozen. Howard had actually called my name. I was a grand finalist! What great insight those judges had!

As I moved gingerly down the risers, I felt a few encouraging pats on my back from the other girls. I strode up beside Howard. For the first time during the entire contest I was giving everyone a genuine smile.

* * *

After we had been ushered off the stage, Wally came running over and gave me a big kiss on the cheek. I pulled away. "Have you gone crazy?" I said, pointing at the cameraman who was following us with a portable unit.

"Oh Carol, I'm so happy for you!" he exclaimed.

"It's great, isn't it?" I yelled, throwing my hands into the air and doing a little dance. "We made it, Wally. We actually made it!"

"Carol," a deep voice called. It was the *Canada Woman* chaperone who had done such a fine job of bawling out the Campbell twins at the museum. "This way, please. You too, son," she said to Wally.

We were paraded past the backstage workers to a hallway off the Simcoe Room and into a private room that had a desk and a mirror with all those fancy lightbulbs around the outside. There was a sofa and a coffee table covered with *Canada Woman* magazines.

The chaperone directed Wally and me to the couch and sat in the desk chair. She had a manila file folder with my name on the index tag under her arm.

"All right," she began, "we've sent for your mom. She'll be back here in a moment."

"She'll be so happy," I said.

"Yes," the chaperone said matter-of-factly. "Now, a couple of things. The talent part of the contest will begin in about one hour. You will be performing last. That is so we can clear everything else off the stage. We have constructed two jumping ramps which we'd like you to check over before they are moved onto the stage. We have also obtained and decorated six barrels."

"Six?" said Wally.

The chaperone looked at him briefly and continued talking. "We have obtained two bicycles"—she checked the folder—"a Mite-E-Max and a Kuwahara. You may choose whichever you wish. Is there anything else you need?"

"How did you get all that stuff?" I asked, puzzled. "How did you know I was going to be chosen?"

"We didn't," she explained. "We assembled all the necessary props and music for all the contestants, just in case. I must say that yours was really the only hard work we had to do. The only other prop anywhere near as cumbersome as yours is a grand piano."

"Wow," I exclaimed. "You certainly are well organized."

"A lot of thought has gone into this contest," the woman declared. "We at *Canada Woman* want to make this the best possible contest, and to get the best possible person to represent Canadian girls during the next year."

"Six cans?" Wally asked again.

"Barrels," corrected the chaperone as she checked the file folder. "According to Ms White you have jumped over five before."

I nodded.

"Obviously Ms White thought you might like to try six. Do you want only five set up?"

"When do I have to decide?" I questioned.

"I suppose right up until the time you jump," she replied.

"I'll let you know," I said.

My mother burst into the room. Her smile stretched from one pierced earlobe to the other. She was shaking all over. "I can't believe it!" She was giggling again. "I can't believe my precious baby is actually a grand finalist in the Ms Teeny-Wonderful contest. I'm so proud. Think of what the ladies' group will say."

"Take it easy, Mom," I suggested.

"Everyone in St. Albert will be watching you. They'll all be cheering for you. Oh Carol, everyone in Edmonton will be on your side. I'm so excited."

"Relax, Mom," I pleaded.

"Just think," she raved on, "you are this close to being the first ever Ms Teeny-Wonderful." She held up a thumb and finger to indicate a very small space. "Carol, you are so close to getting everything you've ever dreamed of. You must be so excited."

Mom definitely needed calming down.

"Mother, will you do me a favour?" I suggested. "I'm going to need my jeans and a sweatshirt for the jump. Will you scoot up to the room and get them out of the suitcase?"

"Jeans?" Mother exclaimed. "I hardly think they'll let you wear jeans in the Ms Teeny-Wonderful contest."

"What am I going to jump in, my dress?" I protested. "Come on, Mom, I need those clothes."

Mother shook her head. "No, dear. Jeans and a

sweatshirt are hardly suitable for a Ms Teeny-Wonderful." She looked over at the chaperone.

"They'll be just fine," the chaperone stated. "Which reminds me of something else. *Canada Woman* insists that all safety precautions be followed. You'll have to wear a helmet and elbow and knee pads, Carol. Any objections?"

"Of course not," I said. "I always jump using Wally's old hockey helmet. It's saved my head more than once."

"Jeans," Mother mumbled in disbelief as the chaperone guided her to the door. "I don't see how that can be right."

"It'll be just fine," the chaperone assured her.

Once Mom had gone on her errand, the large woman turned to Wally and me. "Let's check the ramps and bikes," she suggested.

Again we moved backstage. The area was a hive of activity, but there was nothing to be seen of the other forty-five contestants. No doubt they had been shuffled off somewhere to watch the final scenes.

We came across the bikes leaning against a wall, a silver Kuwahara and a white Mite-E-Max. The Mite-E-Max was a smaller bike. I was anxious to try it out, but I chose the classier bike, the Kuwahara.

The ramps were lying beside the wall. Both had been constructed of two-by-fours and thick plywood. They had been covered with indoor-outdoor carpet. The take-off ramp was about thirty centimetres higher than the barrels we could see further along the wall.

"Incredible!" said Wally in disbelief.

"Is something wrong?" The chaperone flashed us a concerned look.

"Not at all," I gasped. "We're used to piling up bricks or boxes and laying a plank on top. This is unbelievable."

"Then it meets with your approval?" she asked.

"Perfect," I said. "Absolutely perfect."

"Good," she said. "Shall I set up six barrels then?"

"Please do," I replied, watching Wally shake back his bangs so I could see the concern in his eyes.

Once we had returned to our little dressing room and the chaperone had excused herself to attend to her duties, Wally began to rant at me. "Have you lost a screw or something? You can't jump six cans!"

"Barrels," I corrected him. "And why not?"

"Because you've never done it before. That's one good reason."

"Yeah, but I've never had a carpeted ramp to take off from," I pointed out. "And I've never had a ramp to land on. It'll be a cinch. It's just a matter of flying in midair. I don't even have to worry about the landing."

"Like heck!" Wally scoffed, making a fist in frustration. "That nice ramp out there is going to let you take off faster and higher than any of the things we've built. You don't know what that Kuwahara is going to do off it. Plus you're going for a longer distance than you've ever done."

"I almost made six before," I said.

"Sure, with cans. Those barrels look bigger than garbage cans to me."

"Only a little."

"A little can be a lot when you're flying a bicycle." He pounded his fist on the wall. "Carol, what happens if you don't make the distance? What if you land into the ramp instead of on it? You could destroy yourself."

"It's my talent," I protested.

"Then jump three cans," he shouted. "That takes talent. You can do that every time. Leave the daredevil stuff alone."

"I said I would," I pointed out.

"Then change your mind!" Wally demanded as the door flew open to admit my mother.

"Wally Stutzgummer," she said. "What is going on here? I could hear you yelling outside the door."

"Nothing," Wally muttered, looking cross.

Mom threw my jeans and sweatshirt on the couch. "I still don't think it's appropriate to wear those during the contest, Carol. Are you sure you can't jump in a dress?"

"Positive," I said, giving her an impatient look.

"Are you going to do six then?" Wally asked.

I nodded, expecting another outburst of reason.

Instead he let the anger on his face melt into a soft smile. "I knew you would," he said. "I knew I wouldn't be able to change your mind."

I returned his smile.

"I still don't like it though," he announced.

"A six-canner, Wally," I said. "On national TV. Can you imagine what a chance that is?"

"Yeah," he nodded.

"Doing that jump is worth more than the Teeny-Wonderful thing," I said.

His smile became a grin. "I know," he agreed. "I wish it was me."

"Thanks for caring, Wally," I said.

"Sure," he blushed. "I'm going to go and check out that bike while you're getting dressed. Make sure they put everything together right."

Wally left the room and my mother immediately turned to me. "What was that about?" she demanded.

"Wally's a little worried about the jump," I said.

"Why?" Mother gave me her look of overwhelming concern.

"He wonders about the ramps, that's all," I answered.

"Does he think it's dangerous?" Mom probed.

"No," I lied. "He just wants everything to be as safe as possible."

"How many of those things are you going to jump?"

"Six."

"Six?" she exclaimed. "Isn't jumping six cans very dangerous?"

I shook my head. "No, Mom, I've done it lots of times before."

I knew that I was lying, but I felt it was justified. If Mom knew that I hadn't cleared six before, she would be on my case to change the jump. And right now I had enough to worry about without trying to calm her. I didn't need any extra hassle.

Unfortunately my lie was wasted. "Yes, and you've also hurt your wrist before as well, young lady," Mom began almost before I had finished trying to reassure her. "I don't know if I like this bicycle jumping business."

16
A sticky situation

The chaperone returned and rescued me five minutes later.

"We're ready to start the talent portion of the contest now," she told us. "As I said, Carol, you'll be last. Lucy will be first, Cher second, Susan third, then the twins and finally you. There are monitors set up in the hall if you'd like to watch the others."

"Thank you," I said.

"Good luck," the woman smiled. "I'm looking forward to seeing your jump."

"Thank you," I said again.

Mom and I moved into the hallway and stood near one of the many monitors. Terry Howard was introducing the last part of the Ms Teeny-Wonderful extravaganza.

"Ladies and gentlemen, boys and girls, we come now to the most exciting part of the Ms Teeny-Wonderful contest, the talent presentation. As you know, each candidate was chosen not only for her poise and presentability but also for her special talent. Each of our grand finalists will have two minutes to present her special skill.

"I know," he crooned, "that we are in for a treat. These young ladies have long rehearsed their skills for this moment. I would remind you that our judges will be choosing the winner based on the scores received in the talent contest only. No other marks will be used.

"And now, our first talented Teeny-Wonderful, Lucy Dragrett from Yellowknife."

I was finally able to see Lucy. She was an extremely pretty girl with very striking blue eyes. She walked onto the stage carrying a guitar, sat on a chair in front of a microphone and proceeded to play one of the most haunting pieces of music I had ever heard.

"She's good," I said.

"Um," Mom said absently, probably weighing her bike-jumping daughter against this talented classical guitarist.

There was enthusiastic applause when Lucy had finished. The camera returned to Golden Throat. "Wasn't that wonderful?" he cheered. The audience replied with more applause.

"And now," Howard continued, "another fine example of young Canadian talent. Cher Obediah from Brantford, Ontario, is going to recite her own poem on the joys of school."

I let out an unconscious groan, wondering what someone could possibly say was joyous about school. But the poem turned out to be witty and extremely well presented. This Cher certainly had the voice. Even Golden Throat was put to shame. I shivered, imagining what would have happened if I had had to recite my borrowed poem.

Again there was appreciative applause. I could see my mother's eyes vacantly wondering how I could possibly compete with such obviously superior talent.

Terry Howard was introducing Susan Hopkins' talent in ballet when someone tapped me on the back. It was Wally. He jerked his head quickly to one side, indicating that I should follow him.

I left Mom by the monitor. "What's up, Wally?" I asked.

He walked down the hallway and backstage without saying anything. He led me to the bicycles. The Kuwahara was leaning against the ramps, obviously ready for my jump.

"Come here and take a look," he beckoned as he squatted down beside the front wheel. "Look at the bolts on the forks."

I knelt beside him and looked at the bolts. I reached out and touched them. "What?" I questioned. Everything seemed to be all right.

"They're loose," Wally said. "Somebody has unscrewed those nuts. Not all the way, just enough so that they'll hold up when you pedal, but when you come down on that front wheel after the jump it'll fly off. You'll have a super wipeout."

"I don't believe it," I said. "Maybe whoever assembled the bike forgot to tighten them."

"Come on," Wally snapped, "you know who did it as well as I do."

"The twins. But I can't believe they'd go this far."

"Who else?" Wally said.

I shrugged.

"I'll be back," he said grimly as he stood up.

"What are you going to do?" I asked, full of concern. I didn't want Wally doing anything stupid.

"I'm going to repay them for this."

"Wally," I warned, "don't do something stupid because of this. I'll just use the Mite-E-Max."

"They've got it coming," he growled.

"Wally," I said. "Wally!"

But he was gone, marching out of sight toward the hallway. I had never seen good old Wally march anywhere before.

I could hear the applause that indicated the end of Susan Hopkins' performance. Now there would be a few minutes' pause while a grand piano was moved onto the stage for the twins. On the home version of the Teeny-Wonderful pageant all of the delays would be edited out.

I used the time to carefully check out the Mite-E-Max. The bike was fine and hadn't been tampered with in any way. All the bolts were tight. I wheeled it from backstage to where my mother still stood beside the television monitor.

"What do you have that for?" she asked.

"Just getting used to the feel of it," I replied.

I was still concerned about Wally. I could imagine all kinds of horrendous pictures of him sabotaging the twins. Not that I was sorry for them. I was convinced that one of them or one of their escorts had doctored the Kuwahara, probably Dale. I was furious that they would be so vicious to me, and revenge was a sweet-sounding word. But at the same time, I just wanted to get on with my jump and the contest.

The twins were nasty people, malicious and cruel. They weren't just turkeys or jerks, they were definitely sick people who had a lot of problems that they were going to have to work out sometime in the future. So my fury was tempered with pity for the type of individuals they were. I didn't want Wally doing something that would get him into trouble. The Campbells simply weren't worth it.

Terry Howard's face appeared on the monitor. "Our fourth contestant is, as we have mentioned, two for the price of one. These lovely young ladies from our capital city are about to perform a piano duet. Ladies and gentlemen, boys and girls, Joan and Jean Campbell."

The twins walked out on stage and sat down on their black wooden piano bench. They smiled demurely at the camera and began their piece. I don't know much about music, but I do know that the song was something classical and it was played well. I have to give it to their piano teacher; they had been well taught. All the time they played they made occasional glances at the camera and gave coy little smiles. Their act was polished; they had obviously been advised by a professional performer.

When they finished there was enthusiastic applause from the audience. Their talent had made an impression on many people.

"They were good," remarked my mother. "Very good."

They gave the camera their best perfect-teeth smile, and then the audience witnessed Wally's revenge. The twins pushed the piano bench backward in a coordinated movement, then tried to stand up with the same choreographed motion. As they rose, the piano bench rose with them.

I could see the look of surprise on their faces as the weight attached to their rear ends threw them off balance. A loud ripping sound emerged from the monitor as Joan Campbell's dress tore off from the waist down. There she was on TV in the top half of her classy dress and her underwear.

The change in weight threw Jean backward with

the falling piano bench. When the bench landed shakily on the floor again, Jean continued to tumble. She did a perfect backdive and ended with her head on the floor, her feet stuck up in the air.

There were a few cries from the audience, along with much giggling, as the half-dressed Joan ran crying from the stage without helping her sprawled sister.

"I wonder what happened there?" said my mother in shock.

Wally came ambling slowly down the hallway. He smiled at me, nodding his bangs in a greeting. "Did you see what happened?" he asked.

I returned the smile. "Unfortunate accident," I replied.

"Oh," Wally drawled, "I don't think it was an accident. I just heard that someone put some of that new Super-Cement, stick-anything glue on their piano bench."

"Who would do that?" said my mom in disbelief.

"Don't know," I said.

"Beats me," Wally shrugged.

17
Going for it

Terry Howard spent some time while my equipment was being put on stage trying to reassure the audience.

"It's unfortunate that somebody played that terrible joke," he said carefully, "but the Campbell sisters have no need for embarrassment. As you know, we are taping the Teeny-Wonderful contest to be shown later tonight. Our producers will simply edit the accident from their tape."

There was polite clapping.

Shucks, I thought. It would have been the highlight of the show. I was standing, dressed in my helmet and pads, astride my bike, waiting for old Golden Throat to call me onto the stage for the jump.

Once my jumping equipment had been put in place, I had ridden the bike around the stage and up the ramp to check the positioning and get the feel of it. Everything seemed fine. The bicycle was working smoothly; the ramp had no wobbles or warps.

The only thing that bothered me was the distance between the ramps. The barrels *were* bigger than the garbage cans I was used to. Six of them stretched an awful long way. I stood at the top of the take-off ramp and looked across. In my mind I could picture myself driving the bike straight into the descent ramp. I shivered, but there was no going back now.

As I waited, listening to Howard inform everyone of the Campbells' good fortune, Dale walked up to me. He had an angry look on his face and spoke with his jaw tight.

"That was a dirty trick you pulled," he snarled.

"Tell me about it," I replied in kind. "I suppose what you did to my dress and my bike were just fun."

"You can't prove that," he defended.

"Save me the innocent plea," I said. "I've got a jump to do, and if you continue to stand there I'm going to make tire tracks on your face."

He clenched his fist.

"Cool it," I said quietly. "You're out of your league here."

Wally walked up to me. "You got a problem?"

"Naw," I said. "Dale here was just wishing me luck."

Dale said a few words that I knew existed but had never used, never having been angry enough to have the need of saying them. Obviously Dale felt angry enough.

"Real sweet," I smiled as he left.

"Think we're going to have trouble with them?" Wally asked.

"Not any more," I said confidently.

Wally put his hand on my shoulder. "Good luck, Carol," he said. "This is your big chance. A six-canner. Go for it!"

I nodded and listened to Terry Howard explaining about bike jumping and describing what I was going to attempt to do. There were a few gasps of surprise and concern from the audience. I could imagine my mother sitting out front, wringing her hands and wondering how I had gotten into bike jumping in the first place.

Howard's voice had more urgency. "So, ladies and gentlemen, boys and girls, we introduce Carol Weatherspoon, our last grand finalist. Due to the nature of Carol's talent, we are going to ask everyone to be quiet so she can concentrate on her jump. Take it away, Carol."

I looked at Wally. He gave me a thumbs-up sign and a slight nod. I put my weight on the top pedal and pushed out into the stage lights. The audience applauded loudly, then went silent. I could hear muted whispers far away.

I drove around the barrels and the ramps, giving everything a last once over. The hum of the oversized tires on the painted plywood stage was the only sound I heard now. I glanced in the direction of the audience and gave a smile at the bright footlights. Immediately I felt stupid smiling at nobody. For all I knew the area beyond the lights was merely black space.

I came to a stop in front of the take-off ramp and looked at the green carpet that had been neatly nailed down. I began to back away. I backed about fifteen metres, almost to the curtain. I could hear the minute whirl of the casters on the camera stands, but I took no notice. I blinked hard and pushed my surroundings from my mind.

The ramp stretched before me. The mass of it, its partner and the barrels appeared to take up the entire stage. I took a deep breath, feeling anxiety grip my stomach. It made me want to get off the bike and walk away. I sat on the Mite-E-Max, my hands holding tightly onto the handlegrips, and stared at the take-off ramp.

I must have stayed that way for too long, because I heard a voice. "Carol," it said.

I didn't know who was calling me, but it was enough to get me moving. My left foot pushed hard on the pedal. The bike jerked forward, snapping my head. The noise of the tires and the familiar movement of the bicycle brought a rush that started in my stomach and moved through my entire body. I pedalled with a mad fury toward the ramp.

I was standing up, pedalling with great thigh-thrusts, building up the necessary speed. At that moment I was in the mental state that all bike jumpers crave. I was hurtling toward the ramp, gaining the full speed that my muscles and the bike could achieve. Everything else slipped away. The Ms Teeny-Wonderful contest, the audience, the Campbell twins, the loose bolts—all faded to nothingness. The jump became the only thing. I was in my glory. Time itself seemed to alter, to change from normal into some hyper-slow motion that enabled me to savour the moment.

About three metres from the ramp I sat down on the black vinyl seat, still pedalling strongly but letting the built-up momentum thrust the bike forward.

When the front wheel hit the carpet I stood slightly to absorb the bounce. The Mite-E-Max took the shock without falter. The front wheel stayed in a true line.

The movement up the incline seemed an eternity. My breathing and the low hum of the wide treads on the carpet were the only sounds. The bicycle moved upward, dropping a little momentum but still obediently edging toward the point where there would be no more ramp to ride on, only air.

The bicycle moved past the point of no return. It was too late to stop now, even if I wanted to. A full reverse brake would only slow me enough to drop the bike onto the barrels. I sucked in my breath and concentrated on the blurry front wheel.

A metre. Fifty centimetres. The bicycle moved closer to the canyon. Slow time became slower. Centimetre by centimetre the wheel crawled toward the abyss. Thirty centimetres. Fifteen, ten.

At the instant the front tire left the ramp I stood up and pulled viciously at the handlebars. The Mite-E-Max responded beautifully, gradually passing through a forty-five degree angle so that I stood in midair with the bike almost perpendicular to the ground.

It was an incredible feeling, being suspended in midair clinging to a metal bike with emptiness passing below. Only, of course, there wasn't emptiness. There were barrels. Six of them, with *Canada Woman* painted on them.

One.

The first purple and gold barrel vanished beneath me.

Two.

My left wrist was aching from pulling back on the handlegrips. The weight of the bike and my body pulled the front wheel downward. Gravity demanded its due.

Three.

The front wheel stopped being a blur. I was losing speed.

"Come on," I coaxed.

Four.

The barrel seemed to pass at a snail's pace beneath my pedals.

I'm coming down! I thought. I'm coming down too fast. I should be higher. Desperately I yanked at the grips, trying to pull to a higher elevation. The bike started to shake.

Five.

The rear wheel seemed to almost kiss the barrel. The bike was dragging behind me.

"Come on," I yelled, as if my cheering would change the trajectory of the seemingly doomed vehicle.

Six.

Time stopped.

I was aware of descending, unable to move forward. As I watched the purple and gold barrel crawl with geological slowness, I noticed the cramping of my hands on the grips.

I closed my eyes, waiting for the frame and my body to smash with savage force into the descent ramp. Wally had been right. I was trying too much.

I felt a thud and sensed pressure on the rear wheel. I was surprised that my bike was so high that the back tire had hit first. I had expected the impact around the front sprocket. I tightened my hold, expecting to be whipped forward over the ramp.

The next sensation was a feeling of spinning from the front tire. I opened my eyes and saw green carpet moving at normal speed beneath the tires. I was on the down ramp!

In less than a second I was on the painted plywood of the Ms Teeny-Wonderful stage, pushing backward to brake the Mite-E-Max.

We stopped, the bike and I, near the far curtain, looking dumbly at the fabric.

"I made it," I said softly.

The next thing I felt was Wally's arms around me, hugging me with more strength than I thought he had. Somewhere in the distance I heard clapping and cheering and Terry Howard.

"I'm a six-canner," I said.

"Wasn't that wonderful?" Terry Howard exclaimed.

"You were great," Wally declared.

"I did it," I said.

I turned toward the lights and the audience beyond and gave a stupid, silly grin that brought a round of chuckles and renewed applause. I had done it. I had actually cleared six cans—er, barrels—and I had done it on national TV. It seemed as if I had no control over my body. I shook and shivered with delight.

18
The judges make their decision

We sat in our little dressing room, waiting for the call to the stage to hear the decision of the judges and the announcement of the first-ever Ms Teeny-Wonderful. I had changed back into my less-than-fancy dress and sat chewing vigorously on a piece of gum.

"My heart was in my mouth," Mom confessed. "I had no idea that bike jumping was so—er—dramatic."

"It was a great jump," Wally drawled. "Carol did everything perfect."

"Perfectly," I corrected.

"Huh?"

"I did everything perfectly, not perfect."

"Sure," Wally nodded. "That's just what I said, isn't it? You did it perfect."

"After the thrill of that jump, I'm sure the judges will vote highly for you." Mom smiled, a look of victory already creeping into her face.

"Maybe," I said. In truth, I figured I stood a great chance. The jump had gone well. It had certainly been as impressive as the other girls' talents.

The realization that I was close to winning this Teeny-Wonderful thing gave my heart little flutters. Imagine, just three weeks ago I had protested, complained and scolded my mother for even entering me in the competition. Now here I was almost within reach of five thousand dollars and a year off school.

I chomped on my gum with more vigour.

"I hope you don't go crazy," Wally said out of the blue.

"Pardon?" exclaimed Mother, giving my friend the puzzled expression that she reserved solely for him.

"Carol," Wally explained. "I hope Carol doesn't go insane if she wins."

"What are you talking about now?" I demanded impatiently.

"Well," Wally continued, "studies show that normal people who have wealth, notoriety and fame suddenly thrust upon them often can't control the stress and go bananas."

"Bananas?" Mom said.

"Off their sticks," Wally clarified. "Seems that being changed from just normal, average, day-to-day people into something special throws them into a swan dive."

"I don't think that could happen to Carol."

"Never can tell," Wally insisted. "Some lottery winners who find themselves changed from poor into rich can't hack the pressure. They begin to drink too much and take pills."

"I'm hardly going to do that," I said. "Give it a rest, Wally."

"You're the type," Wally nodded his bangs.

"And how can you tell that?" I asked impatiently.

"Because you're already a little crazy now."

I stood up and glared at him. "What do you mean by that?"

He grinned at me. "Just teasing," he said.

I scowled as a polite knock sounded on the door. Wally opened it and the large *Canada Woman* chaperone beckoned me out. "This is it, Carol," she said. "The judges have made their decision."

* * *

Lucy Dragrett, Cher Obediah, Susan Hopkins, Joan and Jean Campbell and I stood on a slightly raised platform to the left of Terry Howard. We were fidgeting, wringing our hands, making nervous little smiles at one another (of course, the twins and I were careful to avoid all eye contact) and watching the white card that Howard was waving toward the audience.

"The judges have made their decision," he announced. "We now have the name of the first Ms Teeny-Wonderful and the four runners-up. Now I am not going to hold anybody in suspense any longer. I only want to say that each of these girls would make an excellent Ms Teeny-Wonderful."

There was enthusiastic applause from the crowd.

"And," he continued, "each girl, whether she wins or loses, will be able to return home proud of her effort and achievement."

This time there was just polite applause.

Get on with it, turkey, I thought.

"I will read off the names in reverse order so that the last name I call will be the winner of the Ms Teeny-Wonderful crown. Now, ladies and gentlemen, boys and girls, the judges' decision.

"The fourth runner-up is"—Howard sucked in his breath slowly—"Susan Hopkins!"

Susan jumped up and down, pretending that she was happy even though she had lost. We gave her quick nervous kisses as she was escorted from the stage.

"Third runner-up"—again a long pause—"Lucy Dragrett."

Lucy gave a big grin and a nod that showed she wasn't disappointed. We gave her the same quick little kisses. "Good luck," she said to me. "I've heard a lot about you from Archibald. Maybe we can meet after the show?"

I nodded nervously as I watched her being escorted from the stage. Archibald? That must be the Pit's name. So now it was down to the three of us. Four actually, but I viewed the twins as the same creature.

Watching Lucy leave made me feel upset. I had hoped that she would get the crown if I didn't win. Even though I didn't know her, knowing the Pit (Archibald!) made us sort of friends. Now I was stuck with the Campbell twins still firmly in the running.

"Second runner-up," announced Golden Throat with an edge of excitement in his voice now that we were near the final selection. "Second runner-up," he repeated, adding to the suspense, "our twosome, Joan and Jean Campbell!"

I broke into another genuine grin. They had come in third. Not even a close second. I had beaten them!

I grinned stupidly at them, offering my hand in good sportsmanship. Their faces revealed a sense of shock and indignation. They had expected to win, and now they had to walk away knowing that I was still standing out there. I loved it.

"Tough luck," I said insincerely.

"Pig," Joan or Jean whispered at me.

I continued to smile, showing my slightly crooked teeth. "Love you too," I said.

After I had watched the twins exit ungracefully from the stage, I turned to face my one remaining opponent. She smiled at me, her long black hair curling over her shoulders, her mouth making little dimples in her cheeks.

"Good luck," I said.

"And to you," she returned the wishes sincerely. We were very graceful contestants at that stage.

"And now," crooned Howard, "before I introduce the first runner-up, I must make special mention of the importance of the position. If for any reason Ms Teeny-Wonderful cannot complete her obligations during the coming year, our first runner-up will become Ms Teeny-Wonderful.

"So, our first runner-up is"—he lingered, letting everyone savour the tension—"Carol Weatherspoon. Cher Obediah is our new Ms Teeny-Wonderful!"

I leaned over, gave Cher a kiss on the cheek and watched her bounce toward Howard, who put a crown on her and handed her a big pile of those long red roses. The audience was on their feet clapping and cheering, occasionally whistling their support of the judges' decision.

There was a touch on my arm. It was the large chaperone. "Sorry," she said over the noise. "I have a feeling you came really close."

I smiled and nodded. "Yeah," I said. "I gave it a good shot."

She escorted me to the left side of the stage where I was joined by all the other Teeny-Wonderful contestants. I say all, but I noticed that the twins were absent. They had no more cause to keep up their good impression. When Cher had finished doing her Grand Walk in front of the audience and the television cameras, we went out, en masse, to congratulate her.

The sight of forty-seven girls mobbing one blubbering, crowned Teeny-Wonderful was the final shot of the contest. At home the viewers would see us with the credits rolling by.

It had been a successful show.

19
Back to St. Albert

"This is Captain Rodger Boswell speaking. On behalf of the crew, I'd like to welcome you aboard Flight Three Six Nine. We are now flying at forty-two thousand feet above the eastern tip of Lake Superior. Our estimated flying time to Edmonton will be three hours and ten minutes. The temperature in Edmonton is currently twenty-one degrees under cloudy skies."

I sat peering out the window at the large cumulus clouds below. My stomach was a knot of tension, but I was far from my frantic state on the trip eastward.

"It's good to be going home," Wally drawled.

It had been an interesting time in Toronto. Certainly one that would remain with me for a long time, perhaps forever. I'm not sure how long memories last.

The post-competition wind-down had left me with a good feeling. After Cher Obediah had been declared the winner, the tension seemed to ease from the rest of us. I know that it did from me. Instead of contestants, we became just girls from other places, getting to know one another.

There was a short victory celebration for Cher after the contest. I was able to meet with Lucy and we became potential friends, agreeing to write and maybe visit one another in the near future. The Pit and Wally made a similar agreement.

As for the twins, I have no idea what happened to them. They vanished after their defeat. Their disappearance bothered no one.

Irene White passed her congratulations on to everybody. "You certainly were an interesting contestant," she said to me. "And remember, Carol, as runner-up you could become *Canada Woman*'s Ms Teeny-Wonderful if Cher steps down for any reason."

"Perish the thought," Henry Chaple added.

Was I disappointed with the outcome? Yes and no. It always hurts a little to be so close to something and just miss it. But at the same time, I felt that being Ms Teeny-Wonderful might have been a big strain on me. Oh, I don't think I'd go insane the way Wally joked, but acting like a wonderful anything was not really my style. I was looking forward to being Carol again, and to being known as the best jumper in St. Albert, a six-canner. That would be enough.

I looked over at Wally, who was drifting into sleep. Good old Wal had done a lot for me in the past few days, helping me sort out my feelings and repaying the twins for their nastiness.

His head nodded. I watched him for a few minutes to make sure he was asleep. Then I punched him violently on the arm and started shouting in my best panic voice.

"Wally!" I yelled. "Wally, the wing just dropped off the plane. We're going to crash! We're going to crash!" I was so effective I almost scared myself.

The stewardess came rushing down the aisle and Mother stood up, asking what was wrong. I didn't mean to upset any of the other passengers. Anybody who was half awake would have noticed that both wings were intact and the plane was flying on in its usual steady manner.

It was Wally I was trying to impress. His eyes opened wide, and for the first time in a long while I had no problem seeing beneath his bangs. His face turned deathly white and his mouth dropped open in fright. He threw his head downward into his hands as if he expected a crash.

I sat smiling and watching as he gradually became aware that the plane was, in fact, peacefully ripping through the atmosphere. Slowly he turned to look at me. His face was still pale and his hands were shaking.

"What?" he said, swallowing hard. "Why did you yell that? You nearly scared me to death. What got into you?"

"I just wanted to thank you for helping me," I

said patiently. "Didn't want you to think that I didn't appreciate you."

As he sat looking at me in disbelief I turned to look out the window, just to make sure that the wing really was still attached.